The Teflon Queen

2

A Novel By

Silk White

Good2go Publishing

GOOD2GO PUBLISHING

7311 W. Glass Lane

Laveen, AZ 85339

Copyright © 2013 by Silk White

www.good2gopublishing.com

twitter @good2gobooks

G2G@good2gopublishing.com

Facebook.com/good2gopublishing

ThirdLane Marketing: Brian James

Brian@good2gopublishing.com

Cover design: Davida Baldwin

Typesetter: Rukyyah

ISBN: 978-0985673499

Printed in the United States of America

10 9 6 7 6 5 4 3 2 1

Acknowledgements

To you reading this right now. Thank you for stepping inside the bookstore, stopping by the library, or downloading a copy of The Teflon Queen 2. I hope you have enjoyed this read from top to bottom. My goal is to get better and better with each story. I want to thank everyone for all their love and support. It is definitely appreciated! Now without further ado ladies and gentleman, I give you **"The Teflon Queen 2"**. ENJOY!!!

Chapter 1

"Shit," Angela cursed as she desperately tried to reach her gun that laid on the other side of the car on the floor. The more she tried to reach the gun, the closer she could feel The White Shadow closing in on her. She tried to unbuckle her seatbelt, but the lock seemed to be jammed. Angela quickly flicked out the knife on her wristband as she looked up and saw The White Shadow quickly approaching. She cut the straps from the seatbelt off and scrambled on the floor searching for her gun. Angela knew all about The White Shadow and what he was capable of so she knew time wasn't on her side.

The White Shadow took hurried steps toward Angela's car. He was paid to take Angela out and there was no way he was going to let her out of his sight. It was no way he was going to take it easy on her because she was a woman and it was definitely no way he was going to not fulfill his contract. Just as he approached Angela's car, he stopped in mid-stride when he heard a deep voice yell freeze from behind him. The White Shadow slowly turned around and before him stood an overweight, gray-haired officer. A smirk danced on his lips as he lowered his weapon. When The White Shadow came back up, he quickly tossed a throwing knife into the center of the cop's throat as if he was throwing a dart. The White Shadow bent down and picked up his gun off the ground as he watched the officer gurgle and choke on his own blood. He smiled as he turned back towards Angela's car. *"The Teflon Queen...Yeah Right!"* He thought as he snatched open the driver side door...Empty! The White Shadow snapped his head over to the left and saw Angela on the other side of the highway running away with a slight limp. Without thinking twice, The White Shadow gave chase. He had

Angela in his site and it was no way he was going to let her escape. He quickly took off in a full sprint chasing after Angela.

"Oh my God," Angela huffed. The car crash had bruised or cracked one of her ribs making it hard and painful every time she took a breath. This was the closest to death she had come in her entire life. The hunter had now become the hunted. Angela limped down the muddy hill moving as fast as she could. She was moving at a decent pace, but it wasn't her maximum speed. She had injured her ribs and hip in the car crash, but the stakes were too high for her to stop running. Angela pushed through the pain as she hurried up the steps leading to the train station. She jetted up the steps, looked back, and saw The White Shadow not too far behind. Angela reached the top of the stairs and took off quickly. She quickly cleared the turnstile not bothering to pay the fare it cost to ride the train. The only thing on her mind at that moment was staying alive and making it to see another day.

"Hey ma'am, come back and pay your fare!" An officer who stood in the cut yelled removing his nightstick from his belt. All day he had been waiting for someone to give him a reason to act like an asshole and now was his chance. Just as the officer readied to go after Angela, he saw a white male in an expensive tailored suit hop over the turnstile right behind her. "Excuse me sir!" The officer yelled roughly grabbing the white man's shoulder. The White Shadow quickly spun around and effortlessly snapped the officer's wrist in the same motion. With his other hand, he forcefully jammed his gun in the officer's chest and pulled the trigger three times. He didn't even wait around to watch the officer's body hit the floor.

Angela's body flinched when she heard the three loud shots ring out. She quickly back peddled over behind a thick iron pole trying to hide and blend in with the rest of the commuters.

Commuters were lined up on the platform in single file as the train pulled in making a loud screeching and rattling noise. The White Shadow finally made it downstairs to the platform just as the train pulled into the station. He watched as people fought to exit and enter the train. There were so many people moving around all at the same time that it made it damn near impossible for The White Shadow to possibly spot the Teflon Queen.

"Stand clear of the closing doors." The White Shadow heard the automotive voice announce through the trains speaker. He only had a split second to decide on whether or not he was going to board the train. After a brief second, The White Shadow quickly slid onto the train just as the doors closed.

The White Shadow flexed his fingers inside his black leather gloves and pulled his Berretta from his holster just as the train pulled away from the station. His gut told him that the Teflon Queen was somewhere on the train and he wasn't going to stop until he tracked her down... The hunt had officially begun.

* * * *

Agent James Carter flew down the street in his car with the siren blasting. He still couldn't believe how Angela had played him for a fool and then turned around and tried to kill him. Part of him still loved Angela while the other part of him hated her and wanted to kill her for deceiving him. When James Carter looked in Angela's eyes right before the mystery man in the suit and black gloves busted into the house, all he saw in Angela's eyes was love, but now all that love had went straight out the window. Angela was now a wanted woman and it was Agent Carter's job to bring in the Teflon Queen; dead or alive. As James Carter flew down the street looking for action, he heard over his Walkie Talkie that shots had been fired and an officer was down at the train station that stood right on the next block. James Carter hit a quick U-turn as he heard the train pass over his head.

"I bet Angela's on that train," he said out loud, as he gunned the engine trying to make it to the next stop before the train did.

* * * *

The White Shadow quickly scanned the train looking for any signs of security or police officers. After a quick observation, he moved on with his mission. Hustlers squeezed by and moved back and forth announcing the different products that they were selling for a small fee. The train was packed. Everyone held overhead rails and the backs of seats to maintain balance. Each and every time the train jerked, it threw passengers into each other. Another woman stood at the other end of the train doing a couple of the latest dance moves for donations. The White Shadow walked past and rudely pushed the lady doing the stupid dance moves out of his was as he hurriedly stepped out of one cart and moved to the next cart while the train was still in motion. The next cart was even more crowded than the previous one. The carriage whined and pitched along the tracks causing all the passengers to sway and rock with the train's momentum. The White Shadow pushed people aside and passed by children whining to their parents and men who were coughing as if they had the flu. He kept an angry, serious look on his face as he headed down the aisle of the crowded train. As The White Shadow moved throughout the carriage, he saw the expression on the faces of the passengers change like night changed to day. With abrupt silence, the crowd tensed. Some of the passengers ducked while others moved away as if a pitbull was on the loose.

They were all terrified and fixated on something behind him. The White Shadow prepared to turn around, but a silenced gun being pressed to the back of his head changed his plans.

"Move and I'll blow your head off!" Angela growled in The White Shadow's ear. "Slowly and I mean slowly drop your weapon down to the floor!"

The White Shadow didn't reply, instead he did just as he was told.

"Kick it!"

"Huh?"

"I said kick it," Angela repeated as she watched The White Shadow kick the gun a few feet away. The gun wind milled on the floor a few times before quickly coming to a stop next to a woman's feet. Most of the passengers yelled as they were trapped on board the Titanic as it was sinking. Others ran away from the two as if their bodies had been strapped with C-4. "Who sent you?" Angela's voice was firm and deadly.

"You already know who sent me Number 2," The White Shadow replied. "You might as well shoot me now," he said in a voice too calm for Angela's liking.

"Oh don't worry, you only have a couple of more minutes left to live, but first I got some questions that need answering." More yells came from the terrified commuters. Angela could tell that they were all praying for the train to hurry up and arrive at the next stop.

"Where can I find Mr. Biggz?"

"Shoot me," was The White Shadow's response.

"You think I'm playing with you?" Angela snarled through clenched teeth.

"Shoot me!" In one quick motion, The White Shadow spun around and grabbed the barrel of Angela's .380. The gun discharged, but not before, he moved himself out of the line of fire. The bullet ripped through The White Shadow's shoulder. The gunshot wound didn't faze or affect him. Actually, it motivated him even more to stay alive. The White Shadow and Angela struggled, fighting for possession of the gun. A vicious battle that neither one wanted to come away the loser of. The gun discharged several more times. Two of the shots hit innocent bystanders, killing them instantly. Screams on top of screams erupted as several commuters scrambled to get out of harm's way. As the two continued to struggle, The White Shadow bent Angela's arm back at the elbow until she finally released the firearm. The White Shadow quickly sprung at Angela and she greeted him with a kick to the gut that took him down to one knee. She quickly grabbed the back of his head and tried to crush The White Shadow's nose in with her knee, but her attempt was blocked. The White Shadow scooped Angela up into the air and tried to forcefully slam her down to the floor, but Angela hung on for dear life as she maneuvered in mid-air and trapped The White Shadow's head and neck in a scissor lock with her legs that quickly took him down to the floor. Angela shot back up to her feet and took off.

The White Shadow snatched his back up 9mm from out of his ankle holster, but by the time he had balance and a steady aim, Angela had escaped into the next car. She fled through the crowd just as the train was slowing down as it approached the next stop.

Angela ducked down as two thunderous shots hit and shattered a window on the train right next to her head. Angela slipped her backup .380 out of its holster and prepared to do battle with the assassin known as The White Shadow. Angela tripped over an older lady that was lying on the floor trying to escape getting killed by all the other passengers that scrambled for their lives once the sound of gunfire erupted throughout the train. Angela crawled over several bodies as she felt the train come to a stop. The doors on the train opened and passengers ran out yelling and screaming as if the train was on fire. Angela stormed out the door, but quickly came to a complete stop when she saw James Carter standing in front of her with his .45 aimed at the middle of her forehead. The thought of pulling the trigger ran through James' mind several times. Just as he built up the courage, he spotted the mystery man about to exit the train.

"Get down!" James yelled. Angela hit the deck and James opened fire. The White Shadow quickly turned to the side behind the body of the train. He stuck his 9mm back down in its holster as he heard bullets bouncing off the train making loud pinging noises. He reloaded his gun then sprung from around the corner ready to open fire, but James was gone.

James could tell from how the man moved that he was a professional. Now he had to find out why this man was after Angela. He didn't know what she was into, but whatever it was it had to be something serious.

* * * *

Angela ran out into the middle of the street and put her hand out as if she had powers to stop cars. A yellow cab came to a screeching halt inches away from Angela's feet. She quickly hopped in the backseat and jammed her gun in the back of the cab driver's neck. "Drive!" Her voice was stern and held a no-nonsense tone. The cab driver thought about it in his head for a few seconds and then placed the gear in drive and pulled off.

"Ummmm...where to Ma'am?" The cab driver murmured softly with a look of fear and nervousness etched across his face.

"Just shut up and drive," Angela barked.

James ran out into the middle of the street and watched as the yellow cab took off.

Angela turned around and locked eyes with James. The look in her eyes told James that she was sorry and never meant for any of this to happen. The yellow cab disappeared around the corner as two loud gunshots brought James back to reality.

James Carter slowly made his way down the train station steps and saw two police officers sprawled out dead on the platform. A small crowd surrounded the two dead bodies. Some of the people were taking pictures and recording the whole incident with their smart phones while others just looked on in shock. There were a few people who screamed and yelled at the top of their lungs turning the situation from bad to worse.

When James reached the crowd, he saw several witnesses pointing in the direction of the dark tunnel. *"Aw shit,"* James mumbled. His job was to take down this crazy killer and try to keep innocent people out of harm's way all at the same time. The last thing he wanted to do was to be down in a dark rat infested tunnel going head up with a professional assassin, but what other choice did he have?

"Here we go," James said to himself. He quickly removed the magazine from his .45 and replaced it with a fresh one. He hopped down onto the train tracks and called for backup. He held his .45 in one hand and a flashlight in his other hand as he went after the man in the tailored suit.

The tunnel was darker than James would have ever expected. The flashlight he held had little to no effect on the darkness. He took cautious steps as he walked through the dark tunnel. He wasn't sure what might jump out at him. With each step he took, James could feel rodents and other creatures crawl and run across his feet and in his path. The further James entered the tunnel, the more noises he heard. Every little sound caused him to turn and aim his weapon in the direction of the noise. To say that James was nervous and scared would be an understatement. He held a firm grip on his firearm. Beads of sweat covered James forehead and face as he followed the beam from his flashlight. A sudden noise caused James to aim his gun and flashlight in the direction that the noise came from. The beam from his flashlight landed on a rat that was the size of a raccoon.

In the rats, mouth was an empty jumbo size potato chip bag. James breathed a sigh of relief. Just as he began to let his guard down, he heard footsteps not too far away from where he stood.

James Carter followed the sound of the footsteps until the footsteps came to an abrupt stop and all that could be heard was a deadly silence. James stopped, squinted his eyes, tried to see further into the darkness, tried to ascertain what lied ahead, weighed the pros and cons of the situation in his head in a matter of seconds, and each second that passed seemed like an eternity. James went to take a step, but froze in mid-stride when he noticed an infrared beam pointed at his foot. The red beam slowly inched its way up from James foot to his leg, his leg to his mid-section, and from his mid-section to his chest where it stopped. Before James could assess what was going on, two powerful blows exploded in his bulletproof vest dropping him off impact. James blinked twice before everything went black.

Twenty minutes later, Agent James Carter sat getting checked on by a paramedic while he looked over Angela's files. "The Teflon Queen," he said loud, as he read over Angela's history of violence. It was sad that after all the time he spent with Angela, he had no clue who she really was. The fact that he was living with the woman who is now on the top ten most wanted list didn't sit too well with him or his boss. James Carter took a deep breath as he sat and pondered on how he was going to catch Angela. After reading Angela's files, he now knew that she wasn't the innocent, little, sweet girl she portrayed herself to be. Instead, she was one of the top assassins in the world. What hurt James the most was the fact that he had put all of his trust into Angela and now he felt stupid; real stupid.

The first thing James had to figure out was how he was going to catch Angela. The second thing he had to figure out was when or if he did catch Angela would he be able to pull the trigger if he had to. His mouth was saying one thing, but his heart was saying something totally different. James Carter knew the only way he was going to catch the man in the tailored suit was if he found Angela before it was too late.

Chapter 2

Angela eased herself down into the tub filled with ice water. Her body was sore and it ached from the run in she'd had with The White Shadow. On top of the toilet seat sat her .380 with the silencer attached to the barrel. Angela didn't know too much about the man they called The White Shadow, but had heard a lot about him and all of his brutal killings. He was at the top of his class and great at what he did. Angela knew from the jump that The White Shadow was going to be a serious problem, a problem that she didn't need right now, and a problem that wouldn't go away until it was buried six feet deep. Angela was sure that everything she had learned about the killing business would be put to the test before it was all said and done. The White Shadow was as sharp as a tack and he was the number one assassin for a reason. Angela was sure she was going to find out just why he was ranked higher than she was.

Angela opened a B.C. powder and downed it with a glass of water. The ice water reduced some of the pain, but not all of it. With The White Shadow on her trail, Angela knew she wouldn't be able to stay in one spot for too long. If she was going to be a target, she planned on being a moving one. Hopping out of the tub, Angela dried off with a towel, and walked around her motel room butt naked. She needed a low-key spot to rest her head while she formulated and came up with her next plan. She quickly slipped on a red lace thong and placed her laptop on the desk. While Angela waited for her computer to boot up, her mind drifted off to James. She hated that things had gone down the way they did, but it was too late to go back and change things now. James was the first man that Angela ever really loved. Even though she knew that she should have never gotten involved with him in the first place. In her mind, Angela wished that somehow, her and James could have figured out a way to make it work where the two of them could have just left town and lived happily ever after, but that was a fantasy. The harsh reality was that the next that time the two of them crossed each other's path sparks would be flying. Not sparks from love, but sparks from a pistol.

Angela continually looked over her shoulder at the door. To say that The White Shadow had her paranoid was an understatement. Angela looked something up on the internet, then quickly hopped up and got dressed. She put on black army pants, a black wife beater, and black combat boots. She placed her custom-made Teflon vest over her head, pulled the straps tight, and snapped the Velcro across her chest. She quickly threw a thin, tight-fitting, black long sleeve shirt over her vest, threw on her blond wig, and walked up to the mirror in the bathroom to make sure her blond wig sat perfect on top of her head. She placed a black skullcap on top of her blond wig and last but not least, she put a pair of dark shades over her eyes to help hide her identity.

Angela reached under the bed, pulled out a duffle bag, and sat it on the bed. Inside the bag were several different types of guns along with several other killing instruments. Angela tossed the duffle bag over her shoulder and headed out the door. She needed some answers and she knew just where to go and get them.

* * * *

Mr. Goldberg paced back and forth in his home office as he spoke to one of his high-end clients on the phone. "Yes Capo, I am working on your appeal," he said into the receiver. Mr.

Goldberg was the slickest lawyer in New York City and he always found a way to somehow beat his cases. "Yes I promise I'll be up there to see you next week," he said then ended the call. Mr. Goldberg hit the power button on his phone, cutting it off. His work was starting to consume his life. He badly needed a vacation, but his greediness and love for money kept him working around the clock. Mr. Goldberg exited his office and headed downstairs. He was in desperate need of a strong drink. He mumbled a few curse words to himself as he entered the kitchen and hit the light switch. When the lights cut on, Mr. Goldberg almost shitted on himself. Standing in his kitchen stood Angela dressed in all black with a two handed grip on a .380 with a silencer attached to the end pointed at his face.

"You scared the shit out of me," Mr. Goldberg said with a hand on his chest. "Put the gun down please! My family is upstairs for God sake," he said coolly.

Angela squeezed the trigger and watched as a bullet lodged in the wall inches away from Mr. Goldberg's head. "The next one won't miss," she warned in a stern rugged voice.

Mr. Goldberg raised his hands in surrender. "Take it easy Angela... I'm your friend; remember?"

"Where can I find Mr. Biggz?"

"Your guess is as good as mines," Mr. Goldberg answered quickly. Even if he did know of Mr. Biggz whereabouts, he would rather die before giving him up. Mr. Biggz was a very important man in the underworld. He had power and enough money to buy his own country if he wanted. Everyone who was somebody knew that Mr. Biggz wasn't to be fucked with. For years, he and Angela did business together and things didn't turn sour until Angela didn't complete the contract on Agent James Carter. For Angela's defiance, Mr. Biggz had hired The White Shadow and paid him top dollar to take out The Teflon Queen.

"Last chance," Angela said slowly removing her sunglasses from her face.

"Come on Angela," Mr. Goldberg began. "We both know that…"

Angela hit Mr. Goldberg with a quick rabbit punch, a shock to his temple, and stunned him. This punch turned Mr. Goldberg's legs into noodles. She yanked his shirt and swept his feet from up under him sending him crashing down to the cold tiled kitchen floor. Angela flicked her wrist and a sharp blade instantly appeared in the palm of her hand. That same hand quickly found Mr. Goldberg's throat. She made sure that the knife pinched the lawyers neck just enough to draw blood.

"Alright! Alright!" Mr. Goldberg squealed with fear and desperation in his voice. He silently prayed to God that his wife didn't come downstairs. "I don't know where Mr. Biggz lays his head. No one does."

"Well you better give me something!"

"I have a number for him," Mr. Goldberg confessed. He had to give Angela something. If not, he was sure she would kill him and his entire family and that was a chance he wasn't willing to take.

"Call him for me," Angela said lifting Mr. Goldberg up to his feet. She watched as the lawyer fumbled around with his phone and then finally makes a call.

Mr. Goldberg didn't want to be involved or caught in the middle of this sticky situation, but what other choice did he have? On the fourth ring, Mr. Biggz finally picked up.

"What do you want Goldberg?" Mr. Biggz asked.

The sound of soft music and several women laughing and joking in the background could be heard. "What you calling to squeeze me for some more of my hard earned money or some…"

Angela snatched the phone from Mr. Goldberg's hand. "So this is what it comes down to?"

Mr. Biggz asked, "Number two is that you?" Her silence answered his question. "Listen Angela, don't make this personal. This is just business. You knew the rules to the game before you played."

"All the hits I've did for you and you couldn't let me slide just this once?"

"Sorry Angela but the game doesn't work that way," Mr. Biggz explained. "If you knew you couldn't kill James Carter then you shouldn't have taken the contract."

"I didn't know I was going to fall in love with him!" she yelled. "I thought I could kill him, but I couldn't! Damn, can I have a break?"

"Ain't no breaks in this business Angela. You are a fucking killer and killers like you don't fall in love!" Mr. Biggz barked. "You didn't fulfill the contact and now you have to pay the price. That's just how it works."

"So because I didn't fulfill one contract out of hundreds, I deserve to die?"

"Listen number two, that's not my problem," Mr. Biggz said in a bored tone.

"Well guess what?" Angela said in a stern vicious tone. "I just became your problem.... and I plan on seeing you real soon!"

Mr. Biggz laughed loudly. "Are you threatening me Angela?"

"I don't make threats....I make promises!"

"So that's how you want to play it?" Mr. Biggz asked with his tone changing from playful to serious in just a matter of seconds. The smile on his face now flipped upside down. "I'll tell you what I'mma do since you wanna be a superwoman and a tough guy." He paused for a second. "I'm going to double the price on your head... And since you don't know what to say out that filthy mouth of yours.... I'm putting the same amount on Agent James Carter's head also."

"I'm going to kill you," Angela growled. Her palms got moist and the tone of Mr. Biggz voice made her nostrils flare. He had her ready to kill without thinking twice.

"You ain't the killer that you used to be Angela," Mr. Biggz told her. "You should have retired a long time ago."

"Mark my words.... I'mma see you."

"Yeah in hell!" Mr. Biggz yelled and then hung up in Angela's ear.

Angela tossed Mr. Goldberg his phone, turned, and headed for the exit.

"Where you going?" Mr. Goldberg called out. He liked Angela and knew that more than likely this would be his last time seeing her alive. Inside he felt bad for her and wished it were something he could do to help.

"I have to go protect James," she answered sadly. "It's no reason he should have to die because of me."

"You really love him don't you?"

"More than anything in this world," Angela said and then went out the door.

Chapter 3

"Ooooh Papi," the Dominican Escort purred in ecstasy. Her moans came from a place deep down inside. They started off soft and then they became desperate. The Dominican woman wrapped her arms around The White Shadow's neck and held on for dear life. The White Shadow pulled the Dominican beauty's knees up and put her legs on his shoulders. He effortlessly lifted her up into the air. All she could do was hold on while The White Shadow bounced her up and down as hard as he could. All that could be heard was skin against skin while the Dominican beauty started to scream and holler as if she was being stabbed to death. She dug her nails into his skin, marking his body up. She left red scratches all up and down his back and neck. The White Shadow went deeper and stroked her love tunnel fast. He stroked it more aggressively until her vagina sung a wet tune.

The Dominican beauty bit down on her bottom lip and stared into the eyes of her lover for the night, crystal clear blue eyes, eyes that told her that this man wasn't as innocent or as quiet as he seemed or portrayed to be, and the eyes of a killer.

"Toma! Toma! Toma!" The White Shadow growled telling his Dominican lover to "take this dick" in Spanish. The White Shadow then roughly tossed his sex partner down on the bed. The bed springs whined as the bed adjusted to the woman's weight. The White Shadow quickly mounted her and entered her walls like a man on a mission. He kissed her body, slapped her ass, pulled her long black hair, and spoke dirty to her in Spanish all while enjoying the furnace that was between her legs. The Dominican beauty sweat as if she had been out on a farm working all day. She stopped screaming, closed her eyes tight, and opened her mouth in the shape of an "O." Her face showed a mixture of pain and pleasure at the same time. If the neighbors in the next room didn't know any better, they would have thought a domestic situation was taking place inside their room.

Finally, she spoke again. "Ooooh Papi! Papi... Papi... Dame Mucho! Mucho! Ahhh, ahhh!" The Dominican beauty's legs started to tremble and then her entire body did the same as a violent orgasm erupted between her thighs. The Dominican beauty closed her eyes again as her breathing tensed, her entire body started to tremble, she swallowed hard, panted, looked up at The White Shadow, and called him an animal in Spanish. She smiled and ten minutes later, she was sound asleep.

After a nice hot shower, The White Shadow walked around his $1200.00 a night hotel room in nothing but a towel. He walked over to the closet and removed an all-black expensive suit. The closet contained several tailored outfits all lined in Kevlar. He had high fashion attire shipped straight from Columbia. His suit could be worn out to dinner or on a battlefield. The White Shadow slipped his two 9mm's with suppressors attached to the business end of the guns down into each one of his shoulder holsters. He put a small backup Glock in his ankle holster and clipped several sharp throwing knives to the back of his belt along with several extra clips. If all else failed, his best weapons were his hands and feet. The White Shadow was trained and knew how to take a life more than 250 ways. It was a reason he was called number one and well known in the underworld for being the best contract killer in the business. Every time The White Shadow took a contract, he would go out of his way to show and prove why he was the best at what he did and that's why he got paid the big bucks.

The White Shadow's cellular buzzed indicating that he had a text message. It was time to get back to work. He picked up his cell phone and saw that Mr. Biggz had transferred funds into his account and texted him an address. His cellular buzzed another text message and this time the text was a picture of none other than James Carter.

Immediately, The White Shadow recognized the agent from the train incident and in his world, killing the agent would be easier than stealing candy from a baby. The White Shadow threw on his suit jacket. The expensive all-black custom-made suit was tailored perfectly to his medium build body. He adjusted his slim tie and grabbed his briefcase that stored two types of broken down assault rifles with bullets big enough to chop down trees. The White Shadow pulled out a few bills and threw them on the nightstand for his Dominican beauty. He turned and stared at her perfectly shaped body sprawled across the bed for a few minutes and then left out the door.

The White Shadow tossed his suitcase into the back seat of his 745 B.M.W. He hopped behind the wheel and pulled out into the street like a mad man. He was already rich so he wasn't in the business for the money, but instead he did it for the love of the sport, which made him even more dangerous and ruthless. As he made his way across town, all that was on The White Shadow's mind was murder. He only got called for the big jobs, he never disappointed, and he always fulfilled his contact. As soon as he agreed to take the contact on The Teflon Queen, he did his homework on her. He knew her favorite foods, favorite places to eat, favorite places to shop, and he also knew that the man she had been sleeping with was none other than Agent James Carter. The White Shadow quickly hit the brakes as an angry New York yellow cab driver cut out in front of him and gave him the middle finger. Immediately, The White Shadow knew he wouldn't be in America for too much longer. He hated Americans; especially the ones in New York City. He couldn't stand their nasty attitudes and rudeness. The White Shadow flexed his fingers in his black leather gloves and continued on towards his destination.

Chapter 4

Agent James Carter and a few other agents stood in his home searching through all of Angela's belongings hoping to find something that would lead them straight to her. As James went through all of Angela's things, it brought back all of the good memories the two of them had shared. The Angela that he knew was a sweetheart, an easy person to love, not this ruthless killer that they had made her out to be. The more James thought about it, if Angela was a professional killer then why was he still alive? Certain things just weren't adding up to him. As James searched through Angela's luggage, he came across a picture of the two of them together kissing. He remembered exactly when and where that picture was taken. James stuck the picture down into his pocket. Did he still love Angela? Yes, but would his love for her stop him from taking her down by any means necessary....No!

Agent James Carter had a job to do and he didn't plan on stopping until that job was done. As the other agents searched through his home, they found a chest in the back of one of his closets that was filled with guns, ammunition, body armor, and all types of other killing instruments. The FBI wasn't taking this case lightly. They planned on shooting first onsite. They weren't taking any chances with The Teflon Queen. She was considered armed and very dangerous and every agent had the green light to shoot on site. The more James thought about the situation, the angrier he became and the more he began to hate Angela.

Two hours later, James sat at his kitchen table alone sipping on vodka and orange juice as he tried to gather his thoughts and cope with the situation at hand. He had spent all of his adult life searching for a woman like Angela and now that he had found her, he would more than likely have to kill her and that was eating away at him. James reached for the bottle of vodka, but quickly paused when he heard a noise coming from the back room. He quickly stood up, removed the loose tie from around his neck, snatched his .45 from its holster, and then inched his way back towards the bedroom. James wasn't sure what the noise was, but he planned on finding out. With a strong two-handed grip, and his arms extended, the .45 entered the bedroom first. Immediately, James noticed that the window in his bedroom was wide open. He was sure that he hadn't left the window open himself so that could only mean one thing. He wasn't in the house alone. James went to reach for his cell phone to call in for backup when he felt the business end of a gun being pressed to the back of his head.

"Don't even think about it," he heard an angry woman's voice growl into his ear. "Cell phone and gun," the voice said. "Drop them on the floor now!"

"You're making a big mistake Angela," James said through clenched teeth. His voice was cold and had a mean edge to it.

"Do it now!"

James tossed his gun and cell phone down to the floor and then slowly turned around to face the woman he thought he'd marry someday. "How could you do this to me? I thought you loved me?"

"Back in the kitchen," Angela ordered as she reached down and picked up the .45 and cell phone. She hated to have to do what she was doing, but what other choice did she have?

James walked back over to his seat at the kitchen table and poured himself another drink with his eyes locked on Angela. He sipped his drink with a mean scowl on his face as he continued to stare a hole through Angela. "Kill me!"

Angela looked down at James with a confused look on her face. "What?"

"You here to kill me right?" James said unbuttoning his dress shirt revealing his slightly hairy chest. "Well go ahead and get it over with."

"James you have to listen to me," Angela began. "I never meant for none of this to happen…"

"You never meant for none of this to happen?" James echoed. "You tried to kill me Angela, murder me, and leave me dead in the streets and you got the nerve to say that you never meant for this to happen?"

"It's not like that James," Angela tried to explain.

"Then what's it like? Huh? You tell me what it's like… Matter of fact; I don't want to talk no more. Just do what you came here to do and get it over with." James was done talking to Angela. The more he talked to her, the more he wanted to kill her.

"I'm not here to kill you James. I'm here to protect you."

"Here to protect me?" James laughed. "Protect me from who; yourself? Here I am thinking I found the perfect woman to spend the rest of my life with then you turn out to be a fucking assassin; one of the top assassins in the world might I add," he said giving her a disgusting look as he sipped his drink. "You murder people for a living and now you show up at our... I mean my house talking about you here to protect me. Fuck outta here!"

"Please James, just hear me out," Angela said removing her dark shades from her face so James could look in her eyes and see that she was sincere.

"How dare you come to my home after what you've done to me and have the nerve to ask me to hear you out?" James growled. His face showed that he was more than angry; he was hurt, but the more Angela spoke his anger was beginning to overlap the hurt. As Angela stood before him, James wanted to make love to Angela and kill her all at the same time. He had mixed emotions and mixed feelings. He didn't know if he was coming or going. He wanted an explanation, but he didn't want an explanation.

"Just hear me out James, please!" Angela shouted finally able to get James full attention. "I'm sorry about everything that happened, but we don't have much time. We have to get going. The White Shadow is on his way over here to kill you."

"The White Shadow?" James face crumbled up with confusion. "What's a White Shadow?"

"I don't have time to explain...we have to get going," Angela said nervously.

"I'm not going anywhere with you until you explain everything." James sipped his drink and leaned back in his chair.

"I work for some very important people James," she explained. "I was paid to kill you. At first, I thought I would be able to, but when the time came, I just couldn't do it. I love you James and I'm sorry and since I didn't kill you, my employers have now hired the best assassin in the world to hunt me down and kill me," Angela said with a hurt look on her face. "And now my employers have put a contract out on you to get to me... And I refuse to let you die because of me James. If they want you, then they're going to have to go through me."

James stared at Angela for a second not saying a word. He took a moment to let her words sink in and digest. "And you expect me to believe that?"

"James it's the truth!"

James asked, "So you want me to believe that you're here to save and protect me when you were the one who tried to kill me... Who are you here to protect me from; yourself?"

"No James, I told you they hired an assassin that calls himself The White Shadow to kill you and..."

"Enough with your fucking lies," James barked. He was ready to jump up and strangle Angela with his bare hands, rip her heart out, and put his foot up her ass. He wasn't buying the bullshit story she gave him. She was going to have to come better than that. "Everything you've told me from day one has been a lie."

"James, I'm not lying," Angela pleaded. "I never meant for none of this to happen...I swear I didn't."

"You may not have meant for it to happen, but it did happen." James sipped some more of his drink. "And it happened because *YOU* let it happen."

"Well I'm not going to let *YOU* die and I'm not going to just leave *YOU* for dead," she said drawing out a few of her words for extra emphasis. "I know you might not trust me, but we only have a little bit of time before shit hits the fan."

"Well if you're so worried about my wellbeing then give me my gun back so that I can protect myself," James suggested.

Angela thought about it for a second. She weighed the pros and cons in her head. She knew that there was a fifty percent chance of James taking the gun and putting a bullet right between her eyes, but with time working against her she had to make a quick decision. Angela holstered her .380, grabbed James' .45 by the barrel, and held it out towards him. "Here"

James grabbed the handle of his .45 and quickly aimed it at Angela's head. "Down on the floor! Now!" he barked. The fun and games were over. He was tired of playing with Angela and most of all; he was tired of hearing all of her lies. James cocked a round in the chamber. "I said now!"

Angela gave him a sad look. "James, I'm not getting down on the floor. We don't have much time…Please let me help you."

"You've helped enough already." James backed up to the house phone that rested on the wall. With one hand, he kept the .45 pointed at Angela's head and with the other hand; he picked up the phone and spoke a few words into the receiver then hung up. "You're going under the jail where you belong."

"If you don't want my help, then fine," Angela said then turned towards the door. "If you want to bring me in, then you going to have to shoot me in the back." Just as the words left Angela's mouth, all the lights in the house went out turning the entire place pitch black. All of a sudden, suppressed rounds tore through the living room windows. All that could be heard was the small crackle of glass raining down on the living room floor. Immediately Angela and James hit the deck and army crawled over towards the stairs. James was seeing first hand that shit could get real, real fast. Once the gunfire stopped, two canisters came crashing through what was left of the living room window. Angela looked back and stared at the two canisters. "Shit!" she cursed as she watched a grenade land on the living room floor. Before she had a chance to do anything else, the two canisters exploded filling the entire house with teargas. Angela grabbed a hold of James and rushed him up the stairs. Angela and James made it halfway up the stairs when a loud blast erupted. The force from the explosion tossed both of them up the remainder of the stairs crashing into a wall.

"Fuck!" Angela winced in pain. She stared up at the ceiling dazed. A cloudy fog of smoke burned her eyes. For a second she couldn't recollect what had happened or where she was. Angela turned to her left and saw James lying face down on the floor. He too was just now coming back around. The explosion had left Angela and James ears ringing and disoriented.

The sound of the front door being kicked open, followed by broken glass being crushed under someone's feet snapped Angela back into the right frame of mind. She struggled to her feet and removed her Tech-9 that was strapped down to the small of her back. Angela coughed and wiped the tears from her eyes as she struggled to help James up to his feet. The teargas was quickly taking its toll on the two. As Angela struggled to get James up to his feet, she could hear the sound of the glass crunching getting louder and louder.

"Come on baby, get up! We have to go!" Angela said in a harsh whisper.

Chapter 5

After the front door came crashing open, The White Shadow stepped inside with a gas mask covering his face and an assault rifle with a suppressor attached to the end in his hands. The gas that filled the house made it hard for The White Shadow to see through the fog. He took cautious, calculated steps as he moved through the living room. In the back of his mind, he wondered if Angela was in the house along with James. If so, that would make his job easier. *"Two birds with one stone,"* he thought out loud. With each step he took, glass crunched under his boots. All the smoke from the two canisters of teargas had caused the smoke alarm to go off. The White Shadow ignored the smoke alarm. He kept a tight grip on his rifle while he inched further and further into the house. The sound of a window being broken coming from upstairs grabbed The White Shadow's attention. Before he could make it up the stairs he saw a muzzle flash, followed by a loud series of automatic gunfire. Rat, Tat, Tat, Tat, Tat! The White Shadow hit the ground, rolled, and came up in an attack posture. He aimed his assault rifle and let it bang. The White Shadow squeezed down on the trigger swaying his arms back and forth. He couldn't see his target, but he knew the type of weapon he had was powerful enough to shoot through the thin walls in the house. The White Shadow aimed the assault rifle up the stairs hoping to pick his intended target off. He grunted when he saw another flash followed by the loud sound of machine gun fire. The shots hit the floor and lodged in the wall inches away from The White Shadow's head. Immediately, The White Shadow figured the shots had to come from no other than The Teflon Queen.

Angela rested low with her back up against the wall. She blindly stuck her arm down the stairs and fired the Tech-9. The machine gun rattled in her hand as shell after shell popped out of the top of the gun. Angela had a handkerchief wrapped over her nose and mouth. Her eyes stung and burned as tears streamed down her face. The teargas was finally beginning to take its toll on Angela. Her lungs felt like they were closing up on her making it hard for her to breathe. Angela looked over to her left and saw James climbing out of the window. She took a deep breath, stuck her arm around the corner again, and squeezed down on the trigger. Again, the gun rattled in her hand. Angela quickly shot to her feet and ran down the hall towards the bedroom as bullets ripped through the walls. Drywall, dust, and plaster rained down on top of Angela's head. She reached the bedroom and stuck her head out the window checking to see how far the distance was from the window down to the ground. She looked and saw James down below on the ground with his gun aimed at the house.

Angela climbed up on the window seal and jumped down to the ground landing perfectly on her feet.

Angela grabbed James wrist and jerked him towards her. "Come on! We have to go!" Angela quickly rushed James over towards the stolen Ford Explorer. The two hopped in the truck with urgency. Angela placed the Explorer in drive as the back glass exploded in a spray of glass. First the back glass went and then the back seat windows were next to go.

"Keep your head down!" Angela barked. She roughly grabbed James' head pulling it down towards her crotch as she recklessly pulled out onto the street. The tires on the Ford Explorer squealed as the smell of burning rubber filled the air.

Angela swerved as bullets exploded through the front windshield leaving holes the size of tennis balls.

* * * *

The White Shadow flew up the stairs skipping two at a time. He moved at an aggressive place until he reached the top landing, waiving the business end of his rifle towards the bedroom. The first thing that caught his eye was the window that was left wide open. The White Shadow took hurried steps over towards the window, looked out, and saw Angela and James hopping inside of a white Ford Explorer. With no hesitation, The White Shadow stuck his assault rifle out the window and held down on the trigger. Fire spit out the barrel as empty shell cases hit the floor sounding like a ton of quarters raining down from the sky. The White Shadow waved the rifle back and forth and watched the bullets from the rifle destroy the Ford Explorer as it recklessly pulled out into the street. Smoke swirled out of the barrel of the assault rifle while The White Shadow quickly headed back downstairs. He removed the spent magazine and replaced it with a fresh one.

With a gasmask still covering his face, and an assault rifle in his hands, The White Shadow exited the house and jogged over towards his B.M.W. He reached the luxury car and heard the sound of tires coming to a skidding stop. The White Shadow spun around and saw two police cars sitting idle. Before the officers could even get out of their cars, The White Shadow opened fire on the two police cruisers. The assault rifle bullets ripped through the cars killing both officers as well as destroying the two police cruisers in the process. The White Shadow let the empty clip fall from the base of the rifle and quickly replaced it with a fresh one just as another cop car pulled up to the scene. The White Shadow walked towards the third and final cop car and opened fire. If it was one thing The White Shadow couldn't stand, it was police officers. In his eyes, they were cowards that hid behind a badge and without that badge, they were nothing.

The officer in the third car threw his cruiser in reverse and tried to get as far away from the mad man with the assault rifle as possible, but a couple of rounds from the assault rifle found a home in the officer's body silencing him forever.

The White Shadow then smoothly walked over to his B.M.W. and opened the door. He sat his smoking hot rifle down in the passenger seat, got behind the wheel, and threw the gear in drive and continued his hunt. The Teflon Queen was starting to get on his nerves. She was beginning to become that pesky fly that never seemed to go away no matter how many times you tried to swat it away, but The White Shadow had the perfect flyswatter sitting right in the passenger seat.

Chapter 6

Angela weaved from lane to lane trying to put as much distance as she could between the Ford Explorer and James' house. She knew The White Shadow was the best in the business, knew that time wasn't on her side, and knew that when dealing with a man like him it was either kill or be killed. Angela checked her rearview mirror every few seconds. It was only natural to be nervous and paranoid when the number one assassin in the world was after you.

"What kind of shit are you involved in?" James asked looking at Angela from the passenger seat. This was his first time really seeing her in action and to say he was impressed was an understatement. James had been through all types of training courses and was considered one of the best agents in the world, but compared to Angela his training seemed like child's play.

"I told you I work for some very important people," Angela spoke keeping her eyes on the road.

"Why does this crazy man want to kill you so bad?"

Angela said, "Because I didn't kill you."

"Who hired you to kill me?" James asked curiously.

"Wayne paid my handler and then I was hired to fulfill the contract," she answered. Her eyes were diverting back and forth from the rearview mirror to the road.

"Why didn't you kill me?"

"Because I love you James," Angela replied in a serious tone. James was the first man she had ever loved in her entire life and the first man she had ever let get close to her. This was the first and only contact that she didn't fulfill.

"So you shoot everyone you love?" James asked sarcastically.

"James I said that I was sorry." Angela glanced over at James for a second. "I could have been killed you if I wanted to James, but I didn't because I.... couldn't."

James nodded his head up and down. "I feel you."

"Do you really?"

James said, "Of course I do.... you said you love me right?"

"More than anything in this world," Angela said with her voice full of love and passion. "Why don't we just leave the country and start a new life," she suggested. "I mean I have more than enough money saved away to last us a lifetime."

"Where would you like to move to?"

"You pick," Angela smiled. "Where ever you wanna go," she said excitedly.

"Sorry Angela, but I can't go with you," James said with a hurt look on his face.

"Why not?"

"Bitch cause you going to jail, that's why," James barked aiming his .45 at Angela's head. "Pull over! You are under arrest!"

"James...."

"James nothing," James barked. "I said pull this motherfucker over now!"

Through the rearview mirror, Angela noticed a pair of headlights weaving from lane to lane at a high speed. These same headlights began getting brighter and brighter in the rearview mirror. Whoever was in the car behind them was closing the distance between the two at a fast pace.

"We got company," Angela stated. "Hold on!" She gunned the engine and watched the speedometer rise while the engine roared. Street lamps passed by in a blur and car horns blared as the Explorer zipped by.

"I said pull over now!" James repeated.

"Not now James," was Angela's only response. She vowed to keep James alive by any means necessary and she didn't plan on stopping now. If James wanted to bring Angela in, he was going to have to shoot her. "Roll your window down and get this guy off of our ass."

James turned around and looked out the broken back window. He saw a shiny black on black B.M.W. moving at a fast pace. "Is that him?"

"Yes!"

James hung half his body out the window and pointed his .45 at the B.M.W. He tried to steady his aim, but before he could even get off a shot, the B.M.W. quickly jumped two lanes over.

The White Shadow jerked the steering wheel to the left and jumped over two lanes cutting off other drivers in the process. He snatched the gas mask away from his face and tossed it in the back seat. He locked his eyes on the white Explorer. The White Shadow held the steering wheel steady with his knees, grabbed his assault rifle, aimed it at the Explorer, and squeezed down on the trigger sending bullets flying through his own front windshield.

Angela ducked her head down as bullets made loud pinging noises as they ricocheted off of the Explorer. She looked up and saw the next exit coming up quickly. Angela cut the steering wheel to the right and nearly side swiped a Honda. She ignored the loud blares of car horns and made the exit right on time. Out of nowhere, bright flashing lights appeared in the rearview mirror. "Shit!" Angela whispered as the Explorer did 90 mph off the ramp.

The White Shadow got ready to follow the Explorer off the exit ramp, but decided against it when he saw two undercover cars tailing the Explorer. Instead of following the Explorer, The White Shadow kept straight. He would just have to catch The Teflon Queen another day.

Angela stomped down on the brakes and cut the steering wheel hard to the left. The Explorer fishtailed out into traffic. With the quickness of a cat, Angela chopped James in his throat and hit a pressure point in his neck that knocked him out cold.

Angela quickly hopped out of the Explorer, sent shots from her Tech-9 into the windshields of the two undercover cars, and then quickly took off on foot through the woods. She hated that she had to leave James, but she had no other choice. All he would do was slow her down and maybe even try to take her down and that was a risk that Angela couldn't take right now.

* * * *

Seven minutes later, James was awoken by a bunch of bright lights in his face and around him stood a trio of paramedics. James sat up, looked around, and saw officers getting led through the woods by K-9s. Little plastic cups covered several shell cases spread out on the ground. Once James spotted the white Ford Explorer surrounded by a bunch of agents, it all came back to him and the first word out of his mouth was…. "Angela!"

Lieutenant Jackson approached James Carter flanked by two white men in black suits. "Agent Carter," he began. "What happened?" He asked getting straight to the point.

"The Teflon Queen saved me," James told his boss.

"The same *Teflon Queen* that every agent in the world is looking for right now?" Lieutenant Jackson asked with a raised brow. Agent James Carter was one of his best agents, but lately his decision-making had been a little off.

"Yes she broke into my house and saved me from The White Shadow."

"The White Shadow?" Lieutenant Jackson asked with a confused look on his face. "What does this have to do with The Teflon Queen?"

"He's another assassin that's been hired to kill me and Angela," James tried to explain. "And he's the real deal. If it wasn't for Angela, I would have been…"

"You're suspended," Lieutenant Jackson cut him off. "You're off this case until further notice."

"No you don't understand…"

"This decision is non-negotiable," Lieutenant Jackson barked. "You and this Teflon Queen chick are a little too buddy, buddy for me. For all I know you and her could be in this together."

"Lieutenant," James began. "I'm the best agent you got and you know I won't stop until this case is closed...I'm telling you this White Shadow guy is no joke and if we don't stop him..."

"Why are you still talking to me?" Lieutenant Jackson cut him off again. "I said you're suspended until further notice!"

"This is bullshit!" James growled and then spun off leaving Lieutenant Jackson and the two agents that stood beside him just standing there.

"I think he's helping her somehow," Lieutenant Jackson said turning and facing the two agents. "I want y'all to tail him and see if he can lead us to The Teflon Queen."

The two agents nodded in agreement. Their new assignment was to tail Agent James Carter and see if he'd lead them straight to The Teflon Queen.

Chapter 7

Kim was asked to remove her shoes before walking through the metal detector. Once she cleared the metal detector, she was then frisked by a female correctional officer. Kim sucked her teeth while the C.O. waved the electrical wand over her clothes. Kim loved Capo, but she hated the process and all the bullshit she had to go through just to visit him. The federal prison looked like an old school castle from the outside, but nonetheless this would be Capo's new home for the next few years. No matter how long the ride took, Kim would be making that commute until Capo was released. After the search process was over Kim was finally allowed to enter the visiting room. Immediately, the chatter and noise from the other inmates interacting with their love ones attacked her ears. Kim and Capo weren't a couple or an item, but it was no secret that the two had the hots for one another. Kim wanted to take things to the next level with Capo, but she didn't want to damage what they had by pressuring him. Capo and Kim may not have ever discussed it, but Kim was wifey and she had no problem letting other women know how she felt about Capo. This was Kim's first time visiting Capo in the federal prison. He had just been transferred to the feds straight from Rikers Island and Kim called herself surprising Capo with a visit.

Kim handed her visiting paper to the visiting room officer and stood in front of the desk while waiting until the C.O. told her what seat to sit in. While Kim waited for Capo to come out from the back, she walked over to the vending machines and purchased a few snacks, sodas, and microwavable sandwiches. Kim sat back down at her assigned table and took in her surroundings. Immediately, she took in how strong, muscular, and tough all of the other inmates looked in their tan Dickie's. She instantly began to fear for Capo's safety. Kim knew Capo wasn't a punk, but still she had never seen men this diesel and brolic before in her life. Kim leaned back in her seat and said a silent prayer for Capo as she waited for him to make his way to the visiting room.

* * * *

Capo sat in front of the T.V. watching the news. To say that he was pissed off was an understatement. Capo was a smooth, get money type of dude who liked to do as he pleased, so to be incarcerated was like being in hell for him. Capo sat and listened to the news reporter talk about how dangerous The Teflon Queen was. The reporter also gave a toll-free number for people to call if they happened to see or run into The Teflon Queen. While the reporter spoke, a picture of Angela was posted on the side of the screen with the words "wanted" underneath her photo. All Capo could do was smile. Even though he and Angela didn't see eye to eye in the beginning, he respected her and he definitely respected her gun. Capo was one of the only people to see The Teflon Queen in action, live, and speak about it. As Capo sat looking up at the T.V., he felt a powerful hand disrespectfully tap his shoulder. Capo turned around and saw three Dominican men standing over him with serious no nonsense looks on their faces.

"What up?" Capo asked looking up at the three men.

"Yo, my man," the leader of the pack spoke. On his neck was a tattoo that said Ace. "That's my chair right there B."

"Listen," Capo said standing to his feet. "I ain't with all this musical chairs and shit. If a chair is empty I'm sitting in it…. Point blank!"

"Point blank?" The Dominican man that called himself Ace repeated with a frown on his face. "Nigga you know where the fuck you at right now?" He asked as the three Dominican men surrounded Capo. Before things got out of control a light skin guy with deep waves in his head walked up with several big rough looking black guys. Each man had some type of red article or fabric on.

"What's popping?" The man with the waves spat looking Ace up and down. "Is there a problem over here?"

"This business doesn't concern you Stacks," Ace said sternly. He and his Dominican friends were part of a power gang called "Patria" and in the prison system; the Patria wasn't to be fucked with. "Why don't you and your crew go step off."

Stacks was one of the big Homics in the Blood organization and he heavily promoted violence. Everyone in the jail knew Stacks, knew what he was about, knew the hatred he had towards the police, and knew that nothing went on in the jail without him knowing about it or being involved in it. Standing beside Stacks was his right hand man Hulk. He got the name Hulk because his big muscles had him looking like the Incredible Hulk from the comic books. Wherever you saw Stacks, Hulk wasn't too far behind. "Any business concerning one of the Homies is my business!"

"Oh," Ace said throwing his hands up in surrender. "My bad… I didn't know he was one of the Homies," he apologized. "An honest mistake…no harm, no foul."

"This the Homie Capo Miller; better act like you know," Stacks said in an over aggressive manner.

"I made an honest mistake Stacks," Ace said. "Don't turn this into something crazy." His tone changed from compromising to serious in one second flat. "You already know how we do."

"We turning this into whatever my man Capo wanna turn this into," Stacks huffed. "I'm tired of y'all Patria niggas running around here fronting!"

Before things went any further, Capo stepped up. "Tell you what we gone do," he said. "I'mma let this slide this time, but next time I ain't gone be so nice."

Before Ace had a chance to respond to what Capo said, a beefy white C.O. walked up on the two crews. "Everything alright over here," he asked with a bit of a smirk on his face.

"Yeah we good over here," Stacks spoke up. If the C.O. didn't walk up when he did, Stacks was seconds away from starting a riot.

"Everything better be good over here...I don't want no bullshit going on in here on my watch," the big C.O. said. He then turned and faced Capo. "Hey new guy, you got a visit. You got twenty minutes to get down there before you get caught up in the count."

Capo turned and gave Stacks a pound. "We gone chop it up when I get back," he said and then headed towards the visiting room.

Capo reached the visiting room, got frisked, and then was finally allowed to enter the visiting room.

Capo scanned a few faces in the visiting room before his eyes landed on Kim who sat at a table filled with snacks and a big smile on her face. When Kim saw Capo walk through the door, she quickly stood to her feet and ran towards Capo. Her heels stabbed the tiled floor with each step she took. Heads turned and studied her enormous ass as it shake, jiggled, and rolled.

"Oh my God, I missed you so much!" Kim shouted. She wrapped her arms around Capo and gave him a bear hug. She kissed him, stuck her tongue in his mouth, and sucked on his bottom lip. She kissed him as if she never wanted it to end, as if she loved him.

When Kim finally let up, Capo smiled. "You look good."

Kim blushed and grabbed a hold of Capo's hands while looking in his eyes. "Thank you."

"What you doing up here? I didn't expect to see you for another few weeks."

"I'm sorry, but I was missing you too much," Kim told him. Inside Kim was still a sad that she and Capo didn't leave town before he got locked up. Part of her wished that she could go back in time and change things and make them better. Kim wished she could have somehow helped Capo to have a better life, but here she was sitting across from him in a visiting room at a federal prison. "How they been treating you in here?"

"It's aight," Capo smiled. "Gotta make the best out of a bad situation…it is what it is."

Well I just want you to know that I'll be here with you until they open these doors and let you out," Kim said in a serious manner. She could see in Capo's eyes that he being confined was killing his spirit. She could see that he wasn't his usual happy self, sitting at the table across from her.

"How your paper looking?"

"I'm doing alright." Kim's eyes shot down to the floor. The last thing Capo needed was another thing to be worrying about while he was locked down. Kim wasn't about to add to his stress. "I'm still alive."

"I didn't ask you were you still alive…I asked you how your paper was looking," Capo said reading Kim's body language.

"I mean after all the lawyer fees, my stash is a little low, but we'll be alright," Kim stated plainly. She was from the hood, so if it was one thing she knew how to do it was survive.

"Aight," Capo said rubbing his chin. "I'mma call you tonight. I got a few niggaz that still owe me a couple of dollars. I'll make a few calls and make a few things happen."

"I'm okay."

"Heard anything from Shekia?" Capo opened a bag of chips, took a couple out, and got his munch on.

"Last I heard, she was out in Miami with Scarface," Kim said. "After Bone beat her up and took the package she moved out to Miami. I guess she's done with this street shit."

"That's good. I'm glad Shekia decided to move out to Miami with Scarface. Scarface is a good guy," Capo said sipping on his orange juice. "What's up with that nigga Bone?"

"He got the streets on lock right now," Kim told him. "Since you've been gone, he is really stepping up his game…he riding around in Beamers, Benz, and Bentley's spending money like it's nothing. He going around telling everyone that he made you and if it weren't for him that you'd been dead a long time ago."

"Who's supplying him?" Capo asked. His nostrils flared. His anger was rising with each word Kim spoke. "I know Scarface ain't supplying him no more. So who's supplying him?"

"I think some chick named Pauleena. You heard of her before?"

Capo nodded, "Yeah I heard of Pauleena. I heard she's at war with some fake Black Panther niggaz called The Spades."

"I don't know nothing about that." Kim leaned across the table and kissed Capo on the lips. "I want to fuck you so bad right now," she growled through clenched teeth. "I miss you so much."

"I miss you too baby," Capo smiled. "I promise we going to be alright."

"I know baby. You just be careful while you in here and please try to stay out of trouble," Kim pleaded with him. "I need you back home. The streets need you back home too so please do what you have to do to get home as soon as possible and in one piece."

Capo looked Kim in the eyes, "I got you."

When the visit was over, Capo and Kim kissed, hugged, and said their goodbyes. Capo palmed Kim's ass, told her he loved her, gave her one last kiss, and then headed back to get strip-searched.

Later that evening, Capo sat in the yard along with Stacks and Hulk. Stacks was putting him on. He was letting him know who was who in the jail and how things were run. He told Capo who to fuck with and who not to fuck with, who was official, and who was not official. Capo sat back taking in everything Stacks was explaining to him. While Stacks spoke, Capo watched a few inmates working out and lifting weights while a few other inmates played basketball that looked more like football. Over in another section, a group of Spanish men was over by the handball court getting a game in.

"What's up with that nigga Ace?" Capo asked. "I was thinking about popping on him when we get back."

Stacks sniffed and then spit on the ground. "Nah that ain't gone do shit but start a big ass war and right now that's something that we can do without."

"Ace and them Patria niggaz got a big following behind them," Hulk said speaking for the first time. "If we were to clash with them, shit is sure to get ugly."

Before Capo could respond, he spotted a familiar face standing over in the yard. This was a face he knew well and a face that a lot of people respected.

"Excuse me for a second... I think I see an old friend." Capo stood up and headed over to the other side of the yard. Knowing that all eyes were on him, Capo made sure he put a little extra in his bop. At first, he wasn't sure if the man he spotted from across the yard was in fact who he thought he was, but the closer he got, the more he realized that the man was indeed who he thought he was.

"Yo what's up old timer?" Capo said disguising his voice.

"Oh shit! Capo what's up?" Wayne smiled. The last person in the world he expected to see was Capo. Wayne and Capo had history together. Wayne had taken Capo in when he was a little knuckle headed teenager running around causing havoc on the streets. Wayne taught Capo everything he knew and loved him like a son, but over the years the two's relationship had begun to deteriorate. "What you doing up in here? It's good to see you," Wayne said extending his hand.

Capo looked at Wayne's hand and left him hanging. "It's good to see me?" He echoed. "What's good with you sending them stickup kids to rob me? What's up with that?"

"You violated," Wayne stated plainly. "You were out of control and I had to bring you down to reality for a second. All I told Cash and Dough to do was just rob you and shake you up a little bit. All that other shit, they did on their own."

"I went out and did my own thing, but I never once sent anyone to harm you," Capo pointed out. "That nigga Cash was trying to blow my head off."

"I had nothing to do with that."

"Nothing to do with that?" Capo repeated. "Nigga you the one that put him on me in the first place," Capo said with his voice raising a few octaves.

"Listen Capo," Wayne began. "I taught you everything you know and all I was trying to do was teach you some manners and respect; nothing more, nothing less. Now if you got a problem with that then it is what it is."

Capo smiled. "That's how you wanna play it?"

"Capo," Wayne let out a frustrated sigh. "I got nothing but love for you and beef is the last thing I want with you. I'm not your enemy, trust me I'm not."

"To be honest with you Wayne, I'm not really feeling you right now," Capo said. He and Wayne's eyes were locked on one another. "So just make sure you stay the fuck out of my way because I can't promise you that I won't do something to you."

"Likewise," Wayne replied with a head nod. "Like I said Capo, I'm not your enemy, but just to give you a heads up," he paused. "Cash is in here."

"In where…here? This jail?"

Wayne nodded, "Yup."

Capo's anger rose and his emotions flared. Past feelings were brought back to life. Cash had robbed Capo in front of hundreds of people and embarrassed him. He made him look like a sucker and then he even had the nerve to walk around wearing Capo's diamond studded "C" chain around his neck as if it was his.

"Well you make sure you tell that motherfucker that Capo is in the building and I'mma be sure to run into him." Capo turned and spun off. Evil and negative thoughts filled his mind. He had thoughts of revenge, payback, and murder. The further Capo made it away from Wayne, the more pissed off he became.

"What's good? You aight?" Stacks asked once Capo returned back over to where the rest of the Homies were huddled up.

"Nah, we might have to make a move on a few niggaz up in here," Capo announced. He loved Wayne like a father, but there were just some things that he couldn't let slide; and Wayne setting him up to get robbed was one of them.

Stacks smiled. "Just say the word and it's on."

Chapter 8

James Carter sat inside a booth in the KFC enjoying his meal. In front of him sat chicken, mashed potatoes, wedges, and an iced tea completed his meal. He sat in a booth facing the window. His eyes were bouncing from his tray of food then back up towards the window. Angela's words lingered around in his head. James didn't believe much of what Angela had told him, but the one thing he was certain about was she wasn't the one out to kill him. With the skills that Angela had, James knew that she could have killed him at any given moment and for him to still be alive said a lot.

James didn't know much about this White Shadow guy. All he knew was the man was a professional killer. He was a killer trained to master the art of killing, a killer who killed with no remorse, and a killer that wouldn't stop until his intended target was no longer breathing.

James Carter wasn't too sure of what was going on. All he knew was that someone was out to kill him. A bounty had been put on his head and from what Angela had told him The White Shadow was looking to collect. James' eyes shot towards the front door and he grabbed the .45 that rested in his lap. A family of three entered the eating establishment; a man, a woman, and a child. James eased his hand off of his .45. The fear of not knowing where the next bullet was going to come from tortured him and played with his mind. It made him a nervous wreck and he felt defenseless. There were still a lot of questions that James wanted answers to. He didn't realize that falling in love with a beautiful woman would change his entire world.

James finished his meal, dumped his tray, and then exited the restaurant. His eyes scanned the parking lot; they went from left to right. Once he saw that the coast was clear he moved on towards his car. James took hurried steps not wanting to be caught out in the open for too long. He slid behind the wheel of his car, stuck the key in the ignition, and made the car come to life. He threw the gear in reverse and went to take his foot off the brake pedal and switch it over to the gas pedal, but the barrel of a gun being pushed an inch deep into the back of his head stopped all that.

"Don't make any sudden moves," Angela said in a harsh whisper from the back seat. She quickly removed the .45 from James' waistline. "Drive!" She made sure she kept her head ducked low.

"You got two agents tailing you. Look over to your right. They are in a black Acura."

James pulled out of his parking spot, glanced over to his right, and spotted the black Acura. He pretended to not see it at all, as he pulled out into traffic. "Why do I have agents following me?"

"They want to see if you can lead them to me. They think we're working as a team," Angela told him.

"Why are you here?" Why are you hiding in the back seat of my car?" James asked. His eyes glanced in the rearview mirror. The black Acura was two cars down trying to be inconspicuous, trying to blend in with the rest of the traffic.

"I have to protect you James," Angela replied. "I'm not going to let someone kill you whether you like it or not. I shouldn't have gotten involved with you from the jump. I knew being with a man like you was wrong, but I got caught up in my feelings. My emotions got the best of me and I got caught up in love...in my line of work, I'm not supposed to love. I was taught not to love or show emotions, but when I met you all of that went out the window."

James asked, "Why me? What's so special about me?"

"I don't know," Angela replied honestly. "I can't help who I love James. At first, my intentions weren't to fall in love with you or to be with you, but I guess God had other plans for me, or should I say us."

James pulled into the driveway of his mother's house. She was away for the weekend so James figured he'd stay there for a day or two until he figured out his next move. He pulled into the garage and waited until the garage door closed before he let the engine die.

Angela was the first one out of the car with the business end of her gun still trained on James. Her gun followed James every move.

James slowly stepped out of the car and stared at her for a few seconds. "Now what?"

Angela holstered her weapon. "First thing is trust. If we don't have trust, then we don't have nothing at all. Can I trust you James?"

"I don't know...can you?" Was his reply.

Angela held James' .45 by the barrel and extended it out towards him handle first. "Yes I can."

James stared at the weapon for a few seconds before finally accepting it. For a second, Angela thought that James was going to turn the gun on her, but when she saw him stick the .45 down in his holster attached to his waistband, she breathed a sigh of relief.

James entered his mother's house through the garage. "You hungry?" He yelled over his shoulder.

"Starving," Angela, replied.

James grabbed two wine glasses from the cabinet and sat them on the kitchen table along with a bottle of red wine. He then went back into the kitchen.

Angela sat down at the table, filled her wine glass with red wine, and sipped it slowly as she heard movement coming from in the kitchen. The sound of something frying could be heard followed by the opening and closing of cabinet doors. Angela removed her blond wig from her head and let out a stressful sigh. It had been a tough week and from the looks of things, it was only going to get tougher. Angela let her hair down and removed her combat boots. She took another sip from her glass of wine. She sat back and watched James move around in the kitchen. She watched him prepare something for them to eat. The more Angela watched James, the more she realized how much she really loved him and there was no way she was going to let anything happen to him. Angela wished she could somehow go back in time and change things. She wished she could start all over somehow and right her wrongs, but the reality of the situation was because of her, now a crazed assassin was out to kill her and James and that was just something she had to live with.

James made his way towards the kitchen table with two plates in his hands. He sat a plate down in front of Angela and then helped himself to a seat directly across from her.

Angela looked down at her plate and saw two cheeseburgers. She loved James' cheeseburgers. "Thank you."

James replied with a simple head nod. He grabbed the bottle of wine and filled his glass. A drink was definitely what he needed at the moment. He needed something to calm his nerves. James bit down into his cheeseburger, leaned back in his chair, and stared at Angela for a second. He took a second to admire her beauty. Angela sitting at the table with her hair down reminded James just why he had fallen in love with her in the first place. She was beautiful and most importantly she was a good woman. James didn't know The Teflon Queen, he knew Angela. He knew her sensitive side and what she was like behind closed doors. James took another bite of his burger and stared at Angela closely while chewing his food.

Angela looked up and noticed James staring at her. "What?"

James took another sip of wine and then said, "Were you serious when you told me I could just pick a place I wanted to move to?"

"Yes."

"Can I ask you a question?"

Angela nodded.

"If you love me as much as you say you do… How could you try to kill me?" James asked. He raised his glass up to his lips, took a deep gulp, and waited for Angela's response.

"James," Angela began. "If I really wanted to, I could have been killed you...even when I shot your car up, I made sure that I sent most of the bullets into the body of the car and not your body."

"That's bullshit!" James barked. "You tried to murder me in broad daylight!"

"Listen James," her voice was soft and innocent. "I never meant to hurt you, and if I did, James I'm sorry. I love you. I love you more than anything in this whole wide world and I want you...no, I need you to find it in your heart to forgive me and let me make this right."

"How you going to make this right?"

"By keeping you alive, that's how I'm going to make this right," Angela told him. She knew James was no match for The White Shadow. He was a good agent, but the two types of training just didn't compare. One was trained to protect and save lives while the other was trained to kill and take lives. "I'm going to keep you alive even if I have to lose my own life in the process."

James asked, "So we supposed to just sit around and wait for The White Shadow to come and kill us?"

"No," Angela replied. She didn't like being the prey. She was trained to do the hunting and it was time to turn the tables. It was time to take the pressure off of herself and put it on her enemy. "I'm not sitting around waiting to be killed. The White Shadow doesn't have to look for me no more because now I'm looking for him."

"*We're* looking for him," James corrected her with a smile on his face, a smile that let Angela know that he really did love her, and she was not in this alone.

"No James, this is too dangerous," Angela replied quickly. "I have to do this on my own."

"Well it's not like I can go back to work," James chuckled. "So I might as well help you get this over with at quickly as possible."

"What if something happens to you? I won't be able to live with myself."

"Something happen to me?" James echoed looking at Angela as if she was insane. "My woman is the best assassin in the world and I know I'm in good hands."

"Oh…so I'm your woman now?" Angela asked finishing off the last of her burger.

"You always been my woman." James stood up, walked over, and kissed Angela on the lips. "Go upstairs and get yourself cleaned up while I think about where I want to move to when this is all over with." He smacked Angela on the ass as she walked past him and headed up the stairs towards the bathroom.

James sat back down at the table and refilled his glass with wine. All kind of crazy thoughts were running through his mind. He didn't know why, but he trusted Angela and felt safe when in her presence. James didn't like that Angela had shot him, but at the end of the day, he was thankful that she didn't kill him. Upstairs he heard the sound of the shower cutting on. Old thoughts of him and Angela filled his brain. All the good times they had flashed before his eyes. James didn't know how, but him and Angela was going to get through this. He just hoped that when it was all said and done that he wouldn't be a wanted man or in a grave somewhere. Ten minutes later, James heard the shower cut off followed by movement upstairs. He grabbed the bottle of wine and refilled his glass. He wondered how the journey that lied ahead would play out. James didn't k now much, but the one thing he did know was that this thing was sure to end in a blood bath.

Minutes later, James saw Angela descending the stairs. Her bare feet inched down the steps one at a time with her red nail polish adding life to her toes. She made it to the bottom of the stairs wrapped in nothing but a towel. She had a .380 with a suppressor attached to the end of the barrel in her right hand.

Her hair was wet, only giving her a more exotic look. Angela sat her weapon down on the table and helped herself to a seat. She crossed one leg over the other, revealing a sexy thigh and a strong calf.

"Sorry but I didn't bring an extra set of clothes." Angela picked up her glass of wine and finished where she left off. "I washed my thong and bra out by hand. I left them hanging up in the bathroom to dry. I hope you don't mind."

James nodded. "It's cool."

Angela asked, "What's on your mind?"

"You!"

"What about me?"

"I don't know why I love you so much," James admitted. He felt stupid for loving a killer. All his life, he was raised to put criminals and killers in jail. Now here he was about to risk his life for a woman that not only was a killer, but also tried to kill him once upon a time. Just the thought of that alone fucked with his mind.

"You thinking too much right now." Angela sipped from her glass. "You can't help who you love James. That's not for you to decide."

James let out a frustrating breath. "So what's the plan from here on out?"

"First we're going to go after The White Shadow and try to catch him off guard," Angela told him.

"Then once that's done, I'm going after my old handler."

"Your old handler?" James questioned.

"A man that goes by the name of Mr. Biggz."

"I'll look him up in the system and see what I can find on him." James finished off his glass of wine.

"Thank you."

James stood to his feet, stretched, and faked a yawn. "It's getting late. You can take the couch and I'll take the floor."

"You going to sleep already?" Angela stood to her feet. "No, don't go yet."

"It's getting late Angela and we both have a lot on our plates. We going to need as much rest as we can get," James pointed out. "Tomorrow is another day."

Angela looked James in the eyes and said, "Fuck me James!"

Her words caused James to stop dead in his tracks. He turned and faced her. "You're drunk Angela. Go lie down and get you some rest...like I said, tomorrow is another day."

"Come fuck me James," Angela repeated in a sexually charged voice. "Your pussy misses you."

"Angela..."

"You don't miss your pussy?" Angela cut him off.

"Angela..."

Angela dropped the towel that covered her body down to the floor and took slow and seductive steps towards James.

At the moment, James didn't see The Teflon Queen, he saw Angela, the woman he loved, the same woman who had tried to kill him, and stood before him butt naked at this very moment. James felt a sexual fire building inside of him and old feelings were beginning to resurrect. The bulge in James pants said one thing while his brain was telling him another.

"Fuck me James," Angela whispered as she lifted up on her tippy toes and kissed James. The kiss started out light, but then turned into a long sloppy kiss. Angela and James tongues did a slow dance. Angela kissed James as if she missed him and needed his kisses to stay alive. A soft moan escaped Angela's lips as James lifted her up. She quickly wrapped her arms around James' neck and locked her toned legs around his waist. She made sure their lips never disconnected. James carried Angela back over towards the kitchen table. He moaned loudly as he sucked on Angela's bottom lip as if it was a piece of fresh fruit. James could feel Angela's warm pussy radiating through the fabric of his slacks. The bottle of red wine along with two plates clanked loudly when they shattered down onto the floor. James gently laid Angela down on the table as if she was a newborn baby. He spread her legs apart like the Red Sea. Instantly his mouth began to water at the site of Angela's slightly hairy pussy.

"You wanna taste this pussy?" Angela asked through clenched teeth.

"Yes"

"I can't hear you," Angela taunted.

"Yeees!" James yelled out loud. His dick was so hard that it felt like it was about to break. James hadn't had sex since he was released from the hospital and he couldn't wait to feel Angela's warmth.

"How bad you wanna..."

James cut Angela off and let out a loud animalistic growl. He buried his face in between Angela's legs and sucked on her swollen clit tasting her juices. It had been so long that James had forgotten how good Angela tasted. James held Angela's pussy lips apart with his thumbs while working his tongue overtime. James licked Angela's wet slit slowly as if he was licking melting ice cream.

Angela moaned and then whispered, "I'm about to cum...that's right, eat this pussy... Yes... Yes...Eat this pussy...Eat this pussy..." Angela abandoned her lady like ways, turned into an animal that had just been freed from its cage, became sexual and primal, and moved her hips in an upward thrust. Her juices covered James face and his body language told her that he wanted her to cum, told her that he wanted her to cum in his mouth. James loudly slurped on Angela's pussy until her legs began to tremble and lock around his neck. She let out a loud, long, and drawn out moan as her orgasm erupted.

James continued to orally please Angela. If she thought for one second that he was eating her pussy like a man possessed to just please her, she was sadly mistaken. James licked, sucked, and slurped on Angela's pussy like a maniac. Satisfying his woman was what pleased and turned him on.

After her orgasm, Angela's clit became real sensitive. "I can't take it any more... Please James... That's enough... I can't take it... I can't take it," she purred with her eyes shut tight. Her chest rose then fell as her breathing picked up.

James ignored Angela's pleas. He made her beg. The more she begged, the more it turned him on. James quickly spun Angela over on her stomach. Her upper body rested across the table while her lower body hung awkwardly half way off the table. James grabbed Angela's ankles and pulled them down until her feet touched the floor. He made her lay her breast flat across the table with her legs spread wide. James grabbed both of Angela's butt cheeks and spread them apart.

Desperate moans escaped Angela's lips as she felt James tongue gliding up and down the crack of her ass. Angela's moans told James that she wanted more. James' tongue made circles then moved up and down, and then from left to right. He gave Angela the sweetest torture. She jerked and made sounds that told James she was on fire. Angela's legs bucked and trembled a second time as she panted and made sounds like she couldn't breathe.

James stood to his feet with a sexy smile on his face. He quickly grabbed an armless chair and sat in it. He then motioned with his index finger for Angela to come to him.

Angela shook her head. "No….I can't," she conceded as she leaned across the table trying to catch her breath.

James reached out, grabbed Angela by her wrist, and pulled her towards him. He made her straddle him, and then filled her up. Angela moaned well and long while her pussy was getting readjusted with James' size.

"Ride this dick Mami!" James growled in Angela's ear.

Angela kissed James, sucked on his lips, sucked on his neck, and bit down into his skin. She did that in an attempt to muffle her moans. She moved up and down, going up easy and coming down hard. She did that over and over. James gripped her ass with both hands while Angela moved and rolled her hips each time she went up and down. It was now Angela's turn to please James. She moaned, cursed, and held on to James neck. She mumbled and made sharp noises followed by short words that made no sense and had no meaning.

Angela moved up and down, and fast and hard while trying to catch her breath. She turned and rode James backwards. Her orgasm came hard and fast. It felt like a series of waves. James spanked her ass. He enjoyed her orgasm just as much as she did. He continued to stroke away. James pulled Angela's hair forcing her head to jerk back. She had told him to fuck her and that's just what he planned on doing. James sucked on Angela's neck until passion marks could be seen. He leaned back and enjoyed the view of Angela slowly bouncing up and down on his tool with her ass opening and closing like a butterfly flapping its wings. Angela spun back around straddling James again. She closed her eyes breathing intensely as her body started to tremble. Between Angela's legs was a raging furnace. She growled and challenged James. She wanted all that he had.

James slapped Angela's ass as he met her thrust for thrust until he felt her body start to quiver again.

"I'm cumming... Ah... Ah... Yes.... Yes... Arrgggggggggh!"

At the same time, James erupted inside of Angela. His orgasm was loud and noisy. James growled like a wounded animal until he was completely drained.

When Angela was done moaning and trembling, she stayed on top of James. She took a second to catch her breath.

"I swear to God I love you," Angela whispered. She was out of breath and felt like she had just finished running a marathon. She could feel James' tool turning soft inside of her. Angela slowly eased up off of James lap. The disconnection made a wet sloppy sound.

James slide down off the chair and melted down to the floor. His eyes were closed as his chest went up and down at a slow even pace. Seconds later Angela could hear the sound of soft snores coming from James direction. Angela looked down at James and smiled. He looked so peaceful and so innocent. He was now in a fetal position sleeping like a baby. Angela kneeled down and kissed James on the forehead. She then headed over towards the kitchen table. Angela cleaned up the mess that she and James had made. Once she was done with that, Angela bent down, picked up her .380, and walked her naked body over towards the window. She slightly opened the blinds to where she could see out, but nobody could see in. Her eyes followed and watched each and every car that drove by. Angela was trained not sleep. She was trained to stay awake for as long as she had to or needed to. While James slept, Angela watched over the house and made sure no harm or danger came their way. Angela looked out the window, out into the darkness. What lay ahead scared her and made her nervous. Angela knew just how serious and dangerous going after The White Shadow was going to be and honestly, she wasn't sure that when it was all said and done that she'd be alive to talk about it. Angela looked out the window. She kept her eyes on the two white agents that were paid to tail Agent James Carter. Angela could see her own reflection through the dark window. A naked image of herself with her hair hanging down, with a .380 in her hand stared back at her.

The Teflon Queen...

Chapter 9

The next morning, James woke up and saw Angela fully dressed with a gun in her hand staring blankly out the window. He stretched and heard various joints cracking and popping. "I see somebody's up early."

"Early bird gets the worm," was Angela's response. Her eyes focused on what was on the other side of the window.

"How long you been up?"

"I been up all night."

James asked, "You didn't sleep all night?"

"I haven't been to sleep in over two weeks," Angela told him. "Hard to sleep when you got the best assassin in the world out looking for you along with every cop in the city...sleep is the last thing on my mind right now."

James said, "I understand."

"Get dressed. We have a long day ahead of us."

James stood to his feet. He could still smell Angela's scent all over his body. It was a sweet scent that he could never forget. "What's on the agenda for today?"

"We going to find out where The White Shadow is hiding and smoke him out."

"I doubt if he's hiding," James said honestly. "And how do you plan on finding out where The White Shadow is laying his head?"

"Easy," Angela smiled. "Mr. Goldberg!"

* * * *

James stormed inside the building where Mr. Goldberg's office was located. He walked past the waiting area and headed straight for Mr. Goldberg's office.

"Sir… Sir… You can't go back there unannounced… Excuse me sir!" The receptionist yelled from behind the counter. James ignored the woman who sat behind the counter and continued straight for the back door that had Mr. Goldberg's name written across the top in gold letters. James barged inside Mr. Goldberg's office not even bothering to knock.

Inside his office, Mr. Goldberg sat with his feet kicked up on his desk and his cell phone pressed to his ear. A look of shock flashed across his face when he saw James Carter storm into his office. "Um…I'll call you right back," he said quickly ending the call. "Um…can I help you?"

James grabbed the back of Mr. Goldberg's head and violently slammed it down on the oak wood desk. Mr. Goldberg let out a feminine sound as blood oozed from his nose like a faucet.

"The White Shadow," James growled. "Where can I find him?"

"Huh…what's this all about?"

James slammed Mr. Goldberg's face back down into the top of the desk. A loud, violent bang erupted when the lawyer's face made contact with the top of the desk. "Last time I'm going to ask you," James growled. "Where is The White Shadow?"

"I don't know," Mr. Goldberg cried with his face covered in blood. "Who sent you?"

James slapped the taste out of Mr. Goldberg's mouth as if he was a simple whore knocking him out of his chair. He pounded on the defenseless lawyer kicking and knocking him across the room. He planned on beating him until he finally broke and told him what he wanted to know. "Where's The White Shadow?"

"Do you have a warrant to just be busting in my office?" Mr. Goldberg asked through a pair of bloody lips.

Before James got a chance to hit Mr. Goldberg again, Angela slowly stepped inside the office. In one hand, she held a gun and in her other, she held a hand full of the receptionist hair.

"I'm going to count to ten and then I'm going to start shooting," Angela stated in an even tone.

"What are you on a suicide mission?" Mr. Goldberg asked with a confused look on his face. "Why don't you two go escape to an island somewhere? Leave the White Shadow alone."

"No matter where we go, you know we won't be safe while The White Shadow is still out there."

"Angela I like you, you know that and I don't want to see nothing happen to you, so please just run as far away as you can. You of all people know just what The White Shadow is capable of," Mr. Goldberg said. "Please Angela! It's not worth it!"

"I'm tired of running," Angela replied. "And a psychopath like The White Shadow won't stop hunting us until we're twelve feet under," she pointed out. "Now are you going to tell me where I can find The White Shadow or am I going to have to start shooting?"

Mr. Goldberg slowly peeled himself up from off the floor and stumbled over towards his desk. He grabbed a pen and a sticky note pad. "He's staying down at that new fancy hotel downtown," he said as he scribbled down the address and handed it to Angela. "Please Angela, just let it go."

"I wish it was that simple," Angela said then released the receptionist hair. "And one more thing before I go."

"What's that?'

"I'm going to need Mr. Biggz phone number."

Chapter 10

The White Shadow sat in the booth of the luxury hotel's restaurant that resided right off of the lobby. Tonight he planned on taking the night off so he could get his thoughts together and come up with a bulletproof plan. The Teflon Queen was turning out to be a tougher assignment than he had expected. The White Shadow hated to, but he had to give Angela her props. She was well trained and very intelligent. She was good, but not good enough. By this time tomorrow night, The Teflon Queen would be no more. Tonight The White Shadow's main focus was on a different kind of mission; a mission that if accomplished would lead him into sexual heaven.

Sitting across from The White Shadow was a beautiful woman. The two had met in the elevator and after a short conversation had both agreed to accompany one another to dinner.

"What did you say your name was again?" The White Shadow asked sipping on his glass of water. The woman that sat across from him wore an expensive looking silver gown along with a bunch of accessories to match. One of those accessories happened to be a diamond wedding ring.

The woman chuckled. "Cathy"

"Okay Cathy, I have a question that I just have to ask."

"Sure go ahead," Cathy smiled. It was obvious that the woman who sat across from The White Shadow was high on cocaine. Since the two of them sat down, she hadn't shut up yet.

"What is a beautiful woman like you doing by yourself in a nice hotel like this," The White Shadow asked. On the table before him sat a plate of fried rice, steak, and potatoes.

"My husband is out of town on business; as usual," Cathy smiled. "I swear he loves his job more than me." She laughed, but her eyes told The White Shadow that what she was saying wasn't a laughing matter. Her eyes told him that she hadn't been fucked in months and that her husband hadn't been taking care of his husbandly duties.

"Why would you say something like that?"

"Money, money, money," Cathy said keeping her smile intact. "That's all he ever talks about, all day and all night. Money, money, money. I get tired of hearing about that all day. I like to hear about and do other things too you know," she said with a sexy smirk.

"Oh really?" The White Shadow sipped some of his water. His eyes were alert as he scanned the entrance and exit every few seconds. There was only one way in and one way out. A 9mm with a suppressor rested on his lap. "You like to do other things like what?"

"You know...things," Cathy said. Her body language told The White Shadow that she wanted him bad and wouldn't stop until she got what she wanted. "By the way, what's your name again?"

The White Shadow paused for a second giving himself time to come up with an alias and then said, "Charlie...the name is Charlie."

"You look like a Charlie," Cathy chuckled. "So Charlie, do you like to do other things too?"

The White Shadow wiped his mouth with a napkin and discreetly slipped his 9mm back inside the holster. "Mind coming up to my room for a second? I want to show you something."

"Will it be worth my while?" Cathy countered.

The White Shadow smiled. "Absolutely"

* * * *

Agent James Carter stormed into the luxury hotel on fire. Right now, he was a man on a mission and defeat wasn't an option. He walked past all the rich folks and wondered what it would be like to be rich just for one day. He wondered what it would be like to wake up and just buy anything you wanted.

James quickly cleared his mind of the foolish thoughts when he made it to the counter. Several people stood before James, but he rudely cut to the front of the line and flashed his badge. "Excuse me ma'am. I'm Agent James Carter," he shouted catching the desk clerk off guard. James showed the woman who stood behind the counter a photo of The White Shadow. "This gentleman is occupying a room in this hotel and I need to know what room he's in."

"Sorry sir, but I can't give you that type of information unless you have a warrant," the desk clerk told him.

"This man is wanted on every most wanted list there is," James huffed.

"I'm sorry sir, but if you don't have a warrant then there is nothing I can do for you."

"This man is a killer and everyone in this hotel's lives is in danger if I don't get to this man in time!" James shouted causing a few strange stares from other guest. "Ma'am I really need you to let me know what room this man," he held the picture back up to the clerk's face. "Is in!"

The desk clerk hit the silent alarm underneath the counter just as she was trained to do when a sign of trouble presented itself. "Sir there is nothing I can do for you. Now if you don't leave, I'm going to be forced to call the authorities on you," she threatened.

James thought about cursing the clerk out, but decided against it. He knew going that route would do more damage to the current situation. James looked over towards the elevators and spotted Angela standing over there. She wore a tan woman's business suit with her Teflon gear on underneath and a pair of boots with a short heel adorned her feet. Normally, Angela would have worn her other combat gear, but in such a luxury place like this her outfit would have stood out like a sore thumb and brought unnecessary stares and heat to her and what she was trying to do.

As James stood there in the lobby looking like a tourist surrounded by a bunch of people speeding to go nowhere, he felt a light tap on his shoulder. He spun around and saw an elderly woman standing before him.

"Mind if I take a look at that picture?" She asked as she reached down into her pocket and removed a pair of glasses. James handed the old lady the picture of The White Shadow.

The old lady examined the photo for a few seconds and then said, "I thought that was the same man."

"You know this man," James asked with his voice full of urgency.

"No I don't know him, but he did check into the room right next to mines," the old lady said smiling. "I'm in room 504 and if I'm not mistaken he's in room 505."

"Thank you so much ma'am. Now I'm going to need you to exit the hotel for a while," he said as he pulled out his cell phone and texted Angela the room number.

"Is everything alright?" The old lady asked.

"Yes ma'am," James said as he quickly headed towards the staircase. Once he was sure that the staircase was clear, he quickly headed up to the fifth floor.

Angela hopped on the elevator when she saw James disappear inside the staircase. She made sure she kept her head down so the camera in the corner wouldn't be able to identify her. A blond wig sat on top of her head and a pair of big designer shades covered her face. Angela watched the red numbers above the elevator door ascend until it reached five. Angela stepped off the elevator and posted up until she saw James exit the staircase door on the opposite end of the hall. Once in their right positions, Angela walked over to the fire alarm switch and pulled down on it.

The alarm blared loudly and echoed even louder throughout the hallways. Seconds later, the halls were flooded with people running out of their rooms in a panic. A loud chatter filled the hall to add on to the blaring alarm. Angela removed a

.380 from each one of her holsters as her eyes locked on room 505. James stood down at the other end of the hall with a sub automatic machine gun resting in his hands. His heart was beating a hundred miles per second as the anticipation of what was going to come next sunk in.

* * * *

"Yes Charlie! Yes Charlie Yes!" Cathy screamed loudly. Wildness invaded her and convulsions had her grabbing the sheets. She frowned back at what was going in and out of her and told The White Shadow that she was about to cum. The White Shadow forced Cathy's head down into the white pillow and gripped her small waist with both hands as he plunged in and out of her wetness. Cathy jerked and made sounds that told The White Shadow that she was on fire. He sank deep, came out, and sank deep again. Cathy made weird noises and strange sounds as if The White Shadow's dick was a knife instead of flesh. Cathy lay on the bed on all fours completely naked except for the expensive heels that remained on her feet. The White Shadow went inside her hard forcing her to scoot away. He moved deeper inside her holding her waist making sure making sure he filled her love tunnel. He quickly sped up his strokes and watched as Cathy's ass viciously bounced up and down against his torso. The White Shadow roughly pulled Cathy's long blond hair jerking her head back as he slapped her ass.

"Oh yes Charlie," she screamed.

SLAP

"That's right Charlie! Tear this ass up!"

SLAP

Once The White Shadow felt like he was getting ready to shoot his load, he quickly pulled out of Cathy and moved around on the bed until he was facing her. The White Shadow stood up on the bed, waved his erection in front of Cathy's face, and watched as her eyes and mouth hungrily followed his penis like a puppy following a stick before its owner tossed it for the puppy to play fetch.

Cathy's hands found The White Shadow's erection and quickly began to massage his balls while tongue kissing the head of his dick. She made loud wet sounds as her head slowly bobbed up and down in a deliberated rhythm. Cathy massaged, licked, sucked, spit, and slurped on The White Shadow performing like a porn star.

"Oh shit," The White Shadow groaned. He grabbed the sides of Cathy's head with both hands and forced her head to move faster, much faster. The sound of Cathy's mouth was loud and moved with determination. He moved her hair from her face and held it so he could watch her performance. The White Shadow closed his eyes as if he was praying then grunted and released his fluids as he felt her swallowing.

"Ohhhh my God!" Cathy exhaled loudly as she lay awkwardly across the once made up bed. "Charlie you are an animal!"

The White Shadow didn't respond. He quietly got up and got dressed. The fun and games were over and done with. Now it was time for him to get back to work.

"Oh my God Charlie, what's that gun for?" Cathy asked as she watched The White Shadow slip his arms into his shoulder holsters.

The White Shadow ignored Cathy as he moved around the room. She hadn't shut up since the two had met on the elevator. All he wanted right now was peace of mind.

"Charlie, you don't hear me talking to you?" Cathy barked. "That's real rude you know!"

The White Shadow quickly walked over towards the bed and smacked the shit out of Cathy. The force behind the slap was so strong that it caused Cathy to do a cartwheel off the bed and down onto the carpeted floor.

Cathy looked up at The White Shadow with her hand on her face and a shocked look in her eyes. "How dare you!" She growled. Cathy jumped up to her feet and began to gather all of her things. "I'm going straight to the police mister and yes I'm going to press charges!"

The White Shadow continued to ignore Cathy until the sound of a blaring fire alarm grabbed his attention. Immediately, he knew something was up. The White Shadow quickly removed a silenced 9mm from its holster and eased his way over to the door. He peeked out the peephole and saw pure pandemonium out in the hallway on the other side of the door.

"Let me out of this room right this minute or else I'm going to scream," Cathy threatened. She made sure she looked The White Shadow in his eyes to let him know that she was serious.

The White Shadow opened the room door and forcefully spun Cathy around with his forearm under her chin in a chokehold position.

"Take your fucking hands off of me!" Cathy screamed as The White Shadow forced her out into the hallway using her as a human shield. Out in the hallway people were running around like chickens with their heads cut off. The White Shadow planned on using all of the confusion to his advantage. He peeked from behind Cathy's head looking for anything or anyone that could cause him harm. At the end of the hallway, The White Shadow spotted the agent that he had run into at the train station calling himself being inconspicuous. The White Shadow quickly put a bullet in Cathy's head blowing blood and brain matter all over the walls. In a swift motion, he pushed Cathy's lifeless body down to the floor. He held his 9mm in his right hand and used his left hand to keep his shot steady as he headed straight for Agent James Carter. The White Shadow took hurried steps and blended in with all the other people who were floating in the hallway scrambling for their lives. Once he was in a close enough distance, The White Shadow raised his 9mm and fired off three quick shots in rapid succession. The sound of the suppressed rounds sounded off like hard slaps. The first bullet found a home in James chest taking him off his feet while the remaining two bullets ricocheted off the wall right where James head was a split second ago.

The White Shadow hurried over towards the agent's body when something in his brain told him to turn around. The White Shadow spun around just in time to see Angela only a few feet away with a mean scowl on her face and a gun in each hand. Before he got a chance to react, three powerful shots exploded in his chest sending him crashing violently down to the floor.

Loud screams sounded off as people ran for their lives once they spotted people waving around guns.

Angela looked down and saw The White Shadow laid out in the hallway with his eyes closed. Angela kicked The White Shadow's gun out of arms reach. Then she rushed over to James' side. Angela was used to working alone so going to check up on James was throwing her off of her game.

James laid on the floor clutching his chest. His Kevlar vest took the bullet well, but the impact had him feeling as if something inside of his body had been broken or cracked.

"You alright?" Angela asked kneeling down. Then she grabbed James' hand and roughly jerked him up to his feet. At that very moment, Angela felt that it was time to abort the mission. Going after The White Shadow would have to be something she did alone. She loved James, but he was slowing her down. It was no way Angela would be able to focus on The White Shadow, protect, and keep James alive all at the same time.

"I'm good," James grunted as he looked down at his bulletproof vest.

"Come on, we have to go," Angela said leading James toward the staircase door. The more she stood in the hotel, the more she realized bringing James with her was a terrible idea. James was out of his element right now and in way over his head.

"Wait," James protested. "Did you check and make sure he was dead?"

"Another time," Angela said. She quickly shoved James inside the staircase as three bullets lodged into the staircase door just as it closed.

The White Shadow snatched his backup gun from his ankle holster, rolled onto his stomach, and fired at Angela and the agent from the floor; all head shots. The White Shadow quickly hopped up to his feet with his 9mm gripped tightly in his hands. He busted through the staircase door, looked over the rail, and immediately spotted Angela and James fleeing down the stairs at a quick pace.

The White Shadow stuck his arm over the rail and sent several loud thunderous shots down at the couple until he emptied his clip.

Angela grabbed James and rushed him into the corner and out of the way of The White Shadow's bullets. "We're going to have to split up!" Angela took the machine gun from James' hand and handed him one of her .380s. Angela and James were posted up in the staircase on the second floor. "Listen, I need you to get out of this staircase and go hide somewhere."

"And what about you?" James asked. He didn't want to split up with Angela and be on his own especially with a crazed assassin on his heels.

"Go hide and I'll keep him off your ass," Angela said. "Hide for ten minutes and then get as far away from this hotel as you can."

"How we gone meet back up?"

"I'll find you…that's my job," Angela winked.

"Be careful," James said as he kissed Angela on the lips and then exited the staircase on the second floor. As soon as he stepped foot on the carpeted hallway floor he heard the loud sound of the machine gun going off that he had just given

Angela. The gun sounded off loudly echoing through the closed staircase door. James jogged down the hallway and prayed that Angela would be all right.

* * * *

Angela blindly aimed the sub machine gun up the stairs and squeezed down on the trigger sending bullets in The White Shadow's direction to keep him at bay. She needed to buy herself a little bit more time to come up with an escape route.

Angela flew down the stairs skipping two at a time. She moved at a quick pace despite the fact that the small-heeled shoes she wore slowed her down a notch. When she reached the landing on the first floor, the door busted open and in ran a police officer catching Angela completely off guard. Before Angela had a chance to react, the cop struck her wrist with his nightstick causing her to drop the machine gun.

Angela quickly grabbed the cop by his shirt and shattered his nose with a vicious head-butt then followed up with a sharp knee to the gut. She grunted as she tried to hip toss the cop down the last flight of stairs, but out of desperation the cop held on to Angela's shirt bringing her down along for the ride with him. Angela pulled the cop underneath her and rode the police officer down the flight of stairs. The ride was bumpy, loud, and ugly.

At the end of the ride, the police officer laid unconscious on the bottom landing. Angela hopped up to her feet, nonchalantly stepped over the officer's body, and exited the staircase. Out in the lobby was straight pandemonium. People were screaming and running for their lives as if the building was really on fire. Angela spotted a gang of police officers guarding the exits helping everyone evacuate the building while several other police officers stood guard and alert as if they were looking for someone or something in particular. Before Angela could think of her next move, she felt the barrel of a powerful handgun being pressed to the side of her head. From the corner of her eye, she saw that the man who held the gun to the side of her head was one of the agents who had been tailing James. His partner ran in the staircase that Angela had just come out of. She suspected he ran in the staircase in search of James.

"You're under arrest!" The agent barked in Angela's ear. Angela held her hands up in a surrendering position. "Down on your knees," he ordered. The agent knew just what Angela was capable of so he kept a close eye on her. His first thought was to blow Angela's brains all over the lobby floor, but bringing The Teflon Queen in would look much better to his superior.

"What's this all about?" Angela asked trying to buy time to come up with her next move.

The agent ignored Angela. "Down on your knees now! Last time I'm going to ask you!" The agent's voice held a serious edge to it, which told Angela that he wasn't bullshitting. Just as Angela got ready to get down on her knees, the sound of several loud shots rang out coming from the staircase behind them.

The agent quickly positioned himself in front of Angela so he could see the staircase door that was behind her. He made sure he kept his gun pressed at the center of Angela's forehead. At that moment, the agent looked in Angela's eyes; the eyes of a killer.

Then several more shots rang out. The sounds of the shots were getting closer and closer. For a split second, the agent took his eyes off of Angela and glanced at the staircase door.

Instantly, Angela could see the fear in the agent's eyes. She swiftly swept her hand across the gun while moving her head in the opposite direction at the same time. Immediately, the gun discharged sending a bullet shattering up into the ceiling. Hotel customers screamed, ducked down, rushed, and pushed towards the exits.

Angela grabbed the agent's wrist that he held the gun in and twisted it in an awkward position until she heard a popping sound. Severe pain resided in the agent's blue eyes as his gun fell to the floor. Angela quickly swept the agent's legs from under him and sent him crashing down to the floor. By now all eyes were one her. Angela looked up and saw four officers heading in her direction. She quickly pulled her .380 from its holster in a snapping motion. She took out the first two with headshots; shots that made the officers head explode like a watermelon being dropped from a fifth floor window. Before Angela had a chance to train her gun on the other two agents, two shots exploded into her chest. The impact from the shots took Angela off of her feet. Her Teflon gear that she wore under her clothes stopped the two bullets from penetrating, but the two slugs made her feel like she was being hit in the chest by two fast balls being thrown by Roger Clemons moving one hundred miles per hour.

Before Angela had a chance to regroup, she felt the remaining two officers hop on top of her in an attempt to restrain her. Angela tapped the bracelet that decorated her wrist and instantly a four-inch blade snapped out and rested in the palm of her hand. Angela plunged the blade in and out of the first officer's neck causing warm dark red blood to spill down onto her face. With a thrust of her leg, Angela flipped the severely wounded officer up off of her and then focused her attention on the remaining officer at hand.

Once the officer saw The Teflon Queen stab his fellow officer, he snapped. The officer screamed at the top of his lungs as he began to rain punches down onto Angela's face. Each punch he threw was intended to knock Angela unconscious.

Two of the punches landed square in the middle of Angela's face before she swiftly spun around on her back while still on the floor, gripping the officer's arm in the process. When she came up, she had the officer's arm in an awkward position. Without hesitation, Angela broke the officer's arm at the elbow. Just as the officer let out a loud and painful scream, Angela bent down and smoothly split the officer's throat from ear to ear.

Angela reached down and removed the officer's service .45 ACP from his holster. She snatched the blond wig from her head and tossed it down to the floor. Her face and the top part of her blouse were covered in blood. Immediately, Angela could tell that her nose had been broken, but at the moment, she didn't have time to worry about that. Right now, her mind was solely on surviving by any means necessary.

Angela tried to blend back in with the crowd, but that was easier said than done being that she was the only one in the whole lobby with blood covering her face. Everywhere Angela looked, there were police officers headed in her direction. The only reason they didn't fire was because she was surrounded by so many innocent bystanders. Angela gripped the .45 tightly in her hand, ready to pop off at any given moment. Just as Angela went to make a move, the staircase door busted open in a dramatic fashion. The White Shadow stepped out the staircase with a mean look on his face. His suit jacket had been removed, his well-tailored shirt and vest had blood on them, and the machine gun that Angela had dropped in the staircase rested in his hands.

A small smirk danced on The White Shadow's lips when he saw all the cops scattered around the lobby. He raised the machine gun and fired into the crowd not caring who he hit. The White Shadow held down on the trigger and waved his arms back and forth. He watched as people fell like Dominos.

Angela quickly pushed her way through the crowd and dipped off inside the hotel's expensive restaurant.

The White Shadow held his finger down on the trigger until the automatic weapon was out of bullets. He tossed the smoking gun down to the floor and looked at all the carnage that lied before him. Out the corner of his eye, The White Shadow spotted Angela trying to sneak off into the restaurant that was connected to the hotel. He thought about going after her, but the sound of shattering glass quickly grabbed his attention. When he looked up, he saw several S.W.A.T. team members come crashing through the front door holding up big shields that had the word S.W.A.T. written across it in bold white letters. He then looked up at the ceiling and saw some S.W.A.T. members sliding down from the ceiling on a thin black rope.

The White Shadow smiled, reached and grabbed a smoke bomb from off of his utility belt and tossed it down at his feet. Immediately, his whole body was fully covered in smoke. The act made him look like he had vanished in thin air. The sound of the staircase door opening and closing could be heard. Once the smoke had cleared, The White Shadow was gone.

A big white man walked through the entrance of the hotel and in his hands, he held an M-16 that had been upgraded with all kinds of gadgets. The white man had muscles like Hulk Hogan in his prime. On his head sat a bandanna and his face was covered in war paint. He wore army pants and an army vest.

Attached to the vest were grenades, tear gas, a hunting knife, two backup pistols, extra clips, and a whole bunch of other shit. A knot of chewing tobacco rested in the left cheek of his mouth.

The white man spit on the floor before he spoke. "Listen up!" he barked. "My name is Lieutenant Get the Job Done." He paused. "But you all can call me "The Gladiator," he announced with a serious look on his face. "I'm in charge and my orders are to bring in The Teflon Queen… dead or alive! All of the exits have been covered which means The Teflon Queen is somewhere in this building." He paused again. "Which means we won't be leaving this building until she's either dead or in cuffs," The Gladiator said with a sick smile on his face. "Move out!" He ordered.

Before him or any of his troops got a chance to move out, the sound of loud machine gun fire could be heard coming from somewhere inside the restaurant. Immediately, The Gladiator and a few S.W.A.T. members headed in the direction of the gunshots while a few other S.W.A.T. members split up throughout the hotel.

Chapter 11

Angela kicked off her heels as she moved through the restaurant with a .45 in her hand. She moved with the quickness and agility of a cat burglar until she reached the kitchen. The sign above the door read *"Employees Only."* Angela eased her way inside the kitchen looking for some kind of back or side exit. Her mind was all over the place as she wondered if James was alright or even alive for that matter. She just hoped and prayed that The White Shadow hadn't caught up with him. Angela wanted to save James, but first she would have to save herself if she expected to save anyone else. As she eased her way through the kitchen, she reached a set of double doors. Angela stopped abruptly when she heard a noise coming from the other side of the door. She placed her back to the wall and held the .45 tight in her hands.

Angela slowly peeked through the small squared hard plastic window and spotted four men dressed in S.W.A.T. gear holding machine guns. Their faces were covered in gas masks and their body language told Angela that they meant business.

Angela kept her back pressed to the wall and waited for the four men to make their way through the double doors. Her heartrate picked up as she counted down the seconds silently in her head. Before Angela could finish her count, one of the double doors eased open. The first thing she saw was the business end of a machine gun peeking its way through the door.

Angela swiftly grabbed the nose of the machine gun and raised it. In the same motion, she jammed her .45 into the S.W.A.T. member's mid-section and squeezed the trigger twice.

Once the first S.W.A.T. member went down, Angela quickly turned the machine gun on the other S.W.A.T. members and opened fire. RAT, TAT, TAT, TAT, TAT, TAT, TAT!

The team of four went down like dominos, each weeping in pain and agony. Angela knew that all four of the S.W.A.T. members wore heavy body armor so the chances of them dying were slim. Angela dropped the machine gun down to the floor and quickly picked up the 9mm and stuck it down into the small of her back. Knowing that time wasn't on her side, Angela moved quickly. She ran over towards the sink and hopped up on top of it. Standing up on her tippy toes Angela reached up and pushed in the thin ceiling that was made of sheetrock. She moved it to the side and pulled herself up into the ceiling. Once up in the ceiling, she quickly placed the tiled sheetrock square back in place just as The Gladiator and more S.W.A.T. members entered into the restaurants kitchen.

The Gladiator spotted four S.W.A.T. members sprawled out across the tiled floor. He and his team of S.W.A.T. members eased their way over towards the wounded soldiers. The Gladiator looked down at one of the wounded soldiers and the soldier quickly pointed up towards the ceiling. The Gladiator looked up towards the ceiling, then back down at his soldier, and gave him a head nod.

The Gladiator slung his M-16 over his muscled shoulder, moved over towards the sink, stepped up, and effortlessly removed the thin square of Sheetrock. Without thinking twice, he hopped up into the ceiling, removed a small flashlight from his gear, and continued on with his hunt.

* * * *

James strolled cautiously through the carpeted hallway with a half scared and half-nervous look on his face. All throughout the building, he had been hearing loud gunfire. James wasn't sure what was going on, but he definitely knew that Angela had something to do with the shots being fired. At first, he was worried about Angela's safety, but after giving it some more thought, he wondered if he should be more worried about the other people's safety.

As James strolled down the hall, he heard a noise coming from one of the rooms. The sound of one of the room doors slowly squeaking open caused him to stop and point his .45 at the door. A teenage boy and girl slowly eased out of the room with their hands up in the form of surrender.

James breathed a sigh of relief when he saw that kids occupied the room. "What are y'all doing in there?" he barked. "The whole building has been evacuated."

"Sorry," the teenage boy murmured. "We heard gun shots... And... I... I just figured it.... would... Be.... Best to just... You know... Stay in the room."

"Get up outta here," James shouted. "Where are your parents anyway?"

The teenage boy looked up and said, "Downstairs at the hotel's restaurant."

"Aight y'all get up out of here." Just as the words left James mouth, several S.W.A.T. members rounded the corner with the quietness of a snake. The only reason James noticed the S.W.A.T. members was because their black outfits caught the corner of his eye. Immediately, several infrared beams appeared on his chest and face. James immediately raised his hands in surrender and swiftly stepped in front of the teenage couple. He slowly reached for his badge and presented it.

"Drop your weapon and lay face down on the floor!" One of the S.W.A.T. members ordered with their guns trained on the trio.

"Do what they say," James whispered to the teenagers as he laid face down on the carpet. He looked up from the floor as the S.W.A.T. team inched their way towards him and the teenagers.

Then loud shots came from up above in the ceiling. Bullets tore through the ceiling and found homes in the S.W.A.T. members. James watched in amazement as each one of the S.W.A.T. members dropped one-by-one. Each S.W.A.T. member laid dead on the carpeted hallway floor, all but one. The last soldier standing quickly raised his machine gun up at the ceiling, pulled down on the trigger, and sent a series of shots up into the ceiling. While the soldier fired up into the ceiling, Angela silently dropped down from the ceiling dropping directly behind the last remaining soldier.

Before the soldier even knew what was going on, his head exploded right before James and the teenage couple's eyes. The soldier's body slowly dropped face first down to the floor and behind him stood Angela. Specs of blood covered her face and a smoking pistol rested in her hand. Angela tossed the handgun down to the floor and picked up one of the dead S.W.A.T. members machine gun.

Angela looked up at James and said, "We have to get out of here." Her eyes quickly went from James to the teenage couple. "Where did they come from?"

James shrugged. "I don't know. They came out one of those rooms."

Angela gave the teenage couple a stern look. "You kids get up outta here…. Now!"

James watched as the two teenage kids quickly scampered down the hallway and then disappeared behind the staircase door. Before James could say another word, a strong diesel body building looking white man dropped down from the ceiling with an M-16 in his hands. Standing there stuck like a deer caught in front of headlights, James didn't even feel Angela tackle him inside the room that the teenagers had come out of just as the sound of an M-16 rifle erupted. Holes the size of golf balls decorated the door and walls.

The Gladiator aimed his M-16 at the location he calculated that Angela would be and squeezed down on the trigger sending bullets through the walls. The Gladiator also knew that the sound of his M-16 being fired would lead the rest of the S.W.A.T. members to his location. Once the smoke cleared, The Gladiator took cautious steps over towards the door. He placed his back up against the wall and on a silent count of three, he peeked his head around the corner. As soon as The Gladiator's head inched around the corner, the sound of a machine gun firing could be heard. The Gladiator jerked his head back in the nick of time. He could hear and feel the bullets whizz past his head.

The Gladiator was a warrior and lived for moments and situations like this. Without hesitation, he removed a grenade from off of his vest, removed the pin with his teeth, and then tossed the grenade inside the room. Seconds later a loud explosion erupted and shook the entire floor. The Gladiator then quickly entered the room. The old bang and flash attack was the format that he'd been using for years.

The Gladiator rushed inside the room and stopped when he came across a male's body. From the looks of things, the man that laid before him was still alive. Before The Gladiator could put a bullet in the back of the man's head, a powerful kick to his face staggered him. The Gladiator went to raise his M-16, but a sharp blade cut into his wrist down to the bone causing him to lose the grip on his M-16. The room was still smoky and made it hard for The Gladiator to see. Out the corner of his eye, he saw something glistening moving at a fast speed coming towards his face. The Gladiator easily blocked Angela's knife strike, and then landed a powerful punch to Angela's mid-section. The impact from the punch sent Angela stumbling backwards. Once Angela regrouped, she stood up with a four-inch blade in her hand and a no nonsense look on her face.

A smirk danced on The Gladiator's face as he removed a huge hunting knife that glistened brightly. This was the type of shit he lived for, the type of hand-to-hand combat that he earned his name from.

In a blind rage, The Gladiator went after Angela. She didn't back down. Angela ran straight towards the man that was more than twice her size and weight. The Gladiator tried to jab his knife in Angela's chest, but she swiftly sidestepped the amateur move and sliced The Gladiator's other wrist all in one quick motion. Angela must have hit a nerve because The Gladiator's knife fell from his hand as his entire hand immediately became numb. Angela quickly followed up with a cut to The Gladiator's face. Then she swiped her blade down The Gladiator's chest leaving a nasty looking gash that would require a double-digit number of stitches to close up. Angela could tell that the white man wasn't as good with a blade as he was with a gun and she planned on using that to her advantage.

Not being one to submit, The Gladiator decided to use his size to his advantage. He faked high and went low in an attempt to take Angela down. Angela quickly shut off his take down attempt with a bone-jarring elbow to the side of The Gladiator's head. The blow stunned him, but it didn't take him out. The Gladiator desperately tried to grab a hold of Angela's shirt hoping to maybe turn the scuffle into a street fight.

Angela took a step back, then viciously kicked the white man in his face hoping to break something. She waited for him to stagger back up to his feet so she could finish him off. The Gladiator's military training was no match for The Teflon Queen. She had taken on much bigger and better opponents than The Gladiator in her heydays.

Once The Gladiator made it back up to his feet, Angela ran and went airborne; taking a knee straight to The Gladiator's wounded and fractured face and sending the big man down hard. Angela then kneeled down, lifted The Gladiator's head, and cradled it in her arm. Before she could snap his neck, several S.W.A.T. members stormed in the room with their guns trained on Angela. Several bright red dots danced on Angela's forehead.

"Let him go… Now!" One of the S.W.A.T. members shouted.

Angela slowly released her grip from around The Gladiator's neck and laid face down flat on her chest. Several S.W.A.T. members quickly piled on top of Angela and bonded her hands behind her back with a pair of plastic tie cuffs. The Gladiator slowly rose to his feet with a look of embarrassment on his face. He had underestimated The Teflon Queen due to the fact that she was a woman. He roughly flipped Angela over on to her back and began to violently stomp her head into the floor while the other S.W.A.T. members placed a pair of plastic tie cuffs on James.

"Alright! Already! That's enough!" James yelled as he watched Angela's face repeatedly bounce off the floor each time The Gladiator's boot made contact with her face. The Gladiator stomped Angela out until his leg tired.

"Get this trash out of my sight," The Gladiator barked. His breathing was heavy and his face was a bloody mess. He watched as his soldiers dragged Angela and James out of the room by their ankles. The Gladiator was about to be a hero and the world was about to know him for bringing down the infamous Teflon Queen. Lieutenant Get the Job Done had once again shown why he got the big bucks. "Let's go out here and address the media," he announced as him and the rest of his team exited the hotel and headed straight for the press.

Chapter 12

Scarface sat in his den with his feet kicked up. In his hands, he held a huge wad of cash. A blunt hung from the corner of his mouth as he counted out the money. He was still pissed off at how Bone had disrespected him by putting his hands on his woman Shekia. Scarface had called Bone to try and talk to him like a man, but Bone cursed him out, called him a sucker for love, and then hung up in his ear. He had to pay for his blatant disrespect and he most definitely had to pay for putting his hands on Shekia. In Scarface's eyes, Bone putting hands and feet on his woman was totally uncalled for and unnecessary. Everyone knew how Scarface got down so it was safe to say that Bone had sealed his own death certificate.

Across from Scarface sat his sister Vicky. Vicky was a beautiful inspiring actress who had a lot of potential. Scarface placed two rubber bands on the thick wad of cash, and then tossed the cash over towards his sister.

Vicky caught the money and grinned. "This is a lot of money. What I gotta do for this?" She asked with a raised brow knowing her brother was always up to something.

"I need you to fly out to New York, get up with this guy, and act like you're interested in him," Scarface told her. "Think you can do that for me?"

"Of course I can, but the question is why should I?" Vicky asked curiously. She wanted to know just what her brother was up to and why.

"The guy I want you to show interest in is the same guy that put his hands on Shekia," Scarface said.

"Who? That Bone guy?" Vicky asked with her face crumbled up. "I thought that situation was over and done with. You still focused on that foolishness?"

"You wouldn't understand."

"What happened is over and done with. Let it go Scarface! Shekia ain't worried about the incident no more and neither should you," she told him.

"I can't let someone get away with violating me or one of my loved ones."

"Any reason to just keep this thing going." Vicky shook her head. "You have a beautiful woman, a beautiful home, and more money than you can spend in one lifetime. You have too much good going on to jeopardize it on some street trash like Bone."

Scarface knew everything that Vicky was telling him was right, but he knew if he didn't do something about the Bone situation; the situation would continue to fuck with him. His male ego was beginning to get the best of him. "So you gonna help me or not?"

"How much is this?" Vicky held up the wad of cash with a slick grin on her face.

Scarface said, "That's $12,000."

"Add another $8000 and I got you," Vicky said smiling. She knew that money meant nothing to her brother and figured another eight wasn't going to hurt him or his pockets.

"Now you trying to rob me," Scarface joked. He knew that even if his sister didn't want to do the job for him that she would still do it if it would help her brother out.

"My services cost," Vicky, said holding her hand out rubbing her fingers in circular motions; the money hand signal that everyone recognized.

"Can't you take something off the price since I'm family?"

"Family is family, but this here is business." Vicky got up and kissed her brother on the cheek. "Besides this will be a good way to put my acting skills to the test," she said striking a pose.

"This is serious business," Scarface said with his voice turning into a serious tone. It was all fun and games, but at the end of the day, this was serious business.

"Okay, tell me exactly what it is that you need me to do?" Vicky asked giving her brother her undivided attention.

"All I need you to do is hook up with Bone and get him to trust you," Scarface began. "I'm going to have a team of shooters following your every move and once Bone is alone with you, I want you to slip something in his drink. Once he passes out, you call my goons and they'll take it from there. This mission shouldn't take you more than a week if your acting skills are as good as you say they are."

"A week it is," Vicky said. "This will be a piece of cake. When you need me to head to New York?"

"Forty-eight hours," Scarface said as he noticed Shekia entering the den with a smile on her face.

Vicky said goodbye to her brother, kissed Shekia on the cheek, and then made her exit.

"Guess what?" Shekia smiled.

"What?"

"I got a letter from Capo today," Shekia said excitedly. At the beginning, she didn't care too much for Capo, but after spending time around him and his crew, Shekia realized that Capo was a good guy who just seemed to make all the wrong decisions at the worst times. She was thankful for the opportunity that Capo gave her to make some money whether it was illegal or not. At the end of the day, if it wasn't for Capo, Shekia would have never met Scarface.

"What that nigga talking about?" Scarface patted his thigh signaling for Shekia to sit on his lap.

"Nothing. He said to tell you what's up. He asked how we were doing and that he was sorry for what Bone did to me."

"I'm still going to make him pay for putting his hands on my queen," Scarface said throwing it out there.

"No!" Shekia grabbed Scarface's face and forced him to look at her. "Let it go baby, please just let it go."

"Okay," Scarface said dryly. He knew that Shekia wouldn't understand where he was coming from so it made no sense to continue on with this conversation. Besides that, Vicky had already accepted the cash for the job so nothing else even mattered at this point.

"You promise?" Shekia asked looking Scarface in his eyes.

Scarface kissed Shekia to shut her up. It surprised and caught her off guard. A simple kiss led to Scarface being on top of Shekia and in between her thick thighs. Her breast pressed on Scarface's chest as her legs wrapped tightly around his lower back. Scarface lifted up and removed his clothes in a hurry as if they were burning through his flesh. Shekia removed her attire a little too slow for Scarface's liking so he roughly helped remove the rest of Shekia's clothes from her body. Then he took her right there on the couch, missionary style, face to face, and tongue to tongue.

Scarface rubbed his energy up against Shekia's wetness. He did that repeatedly until Shekia couldn't take it anymore and grabbed his tool and slipped it inside of her.

"Daaaaamn," Shekia moaned good and long. Her moans deepened as her nails dug deeper into Scarface's skin. She closed her eyes as her breathing tensed and her body trembled. Shekia loved having sex with Scarface. He always made sure he fucked her like his life depended on it and he made sure she had multiple orgasms.

Scarface took Shekia in so many positions that she had never seen before. He went inside her warmth at angles that made sex feel brand new. He moved her around until Shekia was on top of him. Shekia moved up and down, going up easy, and coming down hard with extreme force. Her skin slapping against his sounded off loudly as she did that over and over.

While Shekia bounced up and down on Scarface's dick, he roughly grabbed a handful of her hair, licked her neck, and then growled into her ear.

"That's right! Ride this dick!" Scarface growled in Shekia's ear as she continued to bounce up and down moaning loudly.

"You love this dick?"

"Yes," Shekia moaned. "Yes Daddy."

"I can't hear you!" Scarface slapped her ass.

"Yes Daddy!"

"Louder!"

"Yes Daddy!" Shekia screamed out in pure ecstasy.

"This my pussy?"

"All your pussy Daddy... I promise!" Shekia moaned and cursed holding on to whatever she could as she came hard. She tightly held Scarface's neck and buried her head in his shoulder. She sucked on his neck in an attempt to muffle her moans. Shekia made sounds like she was in severe pain.

Scarface kept pumping until he stiffened up and let out a loud grunt. His face was covered in sweat and his breathing was rough and rugged. He lay down on the couch and embraced Shekia as she cuddled up next to him resting her head on top of his chest.

"I love you," Shekia whispered with her eyes closed. Since moving out to Miami with Scarface, her life had did a complete 360 and changed for the better. It was as if Scarface was sent down from Heaven and made and created just for her. She had never been this happy in her entire life and she refused to let anyone or anything come in between her and Scarface's happiness.

"I love you too baby," Scarface told her as the sound of the doorbell ringing echoed throughout the house. Seconds later, Scarface's butler announced his arrival and waited for Scarface's command before entering the den.

"Mr. Scarface," the butler said with a head nod. "You have a visitor here to see you."

Scarface sat up moving at a turtles pace. "I'll be right back baby." He kissed Shekia on the lips and then followed his butler out of the den.

Shekia laid awkwardly on the couch looking stank. Her hair was a mess and not to mention the clothes that she now had on fitted loosely on her after Scarface had roughly stretched out the outfit she wore when the two were getting their freak on. Thoughts of her mother crossed her mind often. Shekia hadn't spoken to her mother since she decided to just up and move to Miami with this mystery man as her mother called him. Ms. Pat might have been a little bugged out, but at the end of the day, she was still Shekia's mother.

Shekia made a mental note to call her mother sometime in the near future, as she got up and decided to go investigate and see what was taking her man so long to make his way back to the den. She walked through the big mansion with a smile on her face. The sexual episode her and Scarface had just finished had Shekia feeling as if she were walking on clouds. Her smile quickly turned upside down when she spotted Scarface in what looked to be a heated conversation with a woman with a body of a stripper and a face that belonged to a cute hood chick.

"Is everything alright, baby?" Shekia asked interrupting Scarface and his lady friend's conversation.

The chick that stood before Scarface turned and looked at Shekia as if she was insane. "Bitch don't you see grown folks talking. I know your mother taught you better than that," she said snidely. Her tone showed no respect. She then turned her attention back on Scarface and shook her head. "These the type of bitches you fucking with now Marcus?" She made sure she used Scarface's real name so Shekia would know that Scarface and her went way back.

"Mya," Scarface sighed and pinched the bridge of his nose. "Don't come up in here disrespecting my company, that's number one. Number two, what do you want?"

"We need to talk," Mya said placing her hands on her hips. "I know I fucked up Marcus, but I was going through a lot at the time and now I'm here to right my wrongs."

"You had sex with another man, left me, and moved to Atlanta with him, and now a year later you pop up at my door talking about you ready to right your wrongs." Scarface had a disgusting look on his face. Mya had played him for a fool and on the inside; Scarface had yet to get over what she had done to him. "If you think you can right that wrong, then you're crazy!"

"How many times have I forgiven you Marcus? Huh." Mya shouted. The question had caused Scarface's eyes to divert to the floor. He knew he had done his fair share of dirt, but in his eyes, he felt that if he cheated he should be forgiven. But if Mya cheated then that was the end of their relationship. The chicks he may have cheated on Mya with were nothing but a fuck. He didn't care about them, nor did he love them, so in his eyes those chicks were just something to do when it was nothing to do.

"You're no angel Marcus! You've cheated on me and I forgave you," Mya said.

"Yeah, but I didn't cheat on you and move to a whole other state with the woman I cheated on you with either," he pointed out. "You are trifling."

"Marcus how could you…" Mya began, then stopped, turned, and caught Shekia looking dead in her mouth. "Damn bitch! Why is you all in my mouth," she barked and then turned back to Scarface. "Marcus you better get this bitch away from me before I get ignorant up in here."

"Too late," Shekia said in a tone barely above a whisper.

"Don't come up in here talking to my company like that," Scarface growled. "Respect my motherfucking house before you get the shit slapped out of you!"

Once he said that, Mya's entire attitude changed immediately knowing that he would make good on the threat. "Calm down Marcus."

"Ain't no calm down," Scarface huffed. "Get up out my shit!"

"Hmmp!" Mya huffed. "Nigga you must got me fucked up… I ain't going nowhere. You better tell that bitch to leave." She nodded towards Shekia.

Scarface's hand shot out in a blur and smacked the shit out of Mya. Then he grabbed her by her hair and shirt, fought, and struggled to throw Mya out the house.

Shekia stood on the sideline and watched the wretchedness take place right before her eyes. A day that had started out good had now turned into a disaster.

After a long tussle, Scarface had finally tossed Mya out of the house, then closed, and locked the front door. Then he turned and looked at Shekia as Mya beat and kicked at the front door. Curse word after curse word could be heard coming from the other side of the door.

Scarface walked over to Shekia breathing heavily. "Sorry about that baby." He went to kiss Shekia on the lips, but she quickly jerked her head back out of range. "What?" Scarface asked with a confused look on his face.

"So I'm just company now?" Shekia asked with much attitude.

"Come on Ma, don't do that."

"I think it might be best if I go back to New York for a while," Shekia suggested. Just when she was beginning to think that Scarface was different, a ratchet chick showed up at his front door disrespecting her.

"Why you acting like that?" Scarface pressed.

"I ain't acting like nothing," Shekia snapped. "One minute you love me so much and I'm your Queen, then as soon as another woman pops up on the scene, I turn into company." She chuckled as her eyes blinked repeatedly trying not to let any tears escape.

"You know I ain't mean it like that..."

"But that's how you said it," Shekia cut him off. By now, the tears were flowing like a river. She tried to storm off to their bedroom to grab a few of her things, but Scarface aggressively grabbed her wrist, abruptly stopping her momentum.

"Wait baby... Don't do this..."

Shekia looked at Scarface and then back down at her wrist that was in his grasp. "Take your hands off me... Now!" she growled before snatching her wrist free. Scarface had let Mya come into their home and disrespect her and Shekia wasn't feeling that. It was already bad enough that she was in a city that she knew nothing about, but to be disrespected on top of that was something that was unacceptable to Shekia.

"Can we talk about this? Please?" Scarface pleaded with his hands in a praying position.

"Ain't nothing to talk about," Shekia barked and then stormed off upstairs. She didn't really want to leave Scarface, but foolish pride played a big part in her decision. In all reality, Scarface was the best thing that had ever happened to Shekia, but the fear of him breaking her heart is what had Shekia thinking the worst. At the end of the day, she had to protect her heart.

Shekia hit the light switch in her walk-in closet and stepped in. Her closet was full of all of the latest designer name brand garments. "I feel so stupid right now," Shekia whispered to herself. She bent down and picked up the Louis Vuitton duffle bag when she felt a pair of hands gently wrap around her waist. Before she could protest, a soft pair of lips slowly sucked and kissed on the nape of her neck.

"I'm sorry Mami," Scarface whispered in between wet kisses. "Please don't leave me... I'll do anything if you stay...

And I mean… Anything," he said making sure he dragged out the end of his sentence letting her know he meant exactly what he said.

"No Scarface… Stop," Shekia whispered with her eyes closed. Instantly wetness formed in between her legs from her man's touch. "Stop baby; please."

"I'm sorry Kia…" Scarface slipped his hands in the front of Shekia's shorts and fondled her clit from behind while whispering in her ear. "What can I do to make you forgive me?"

"No Scarface, you've been a bad boy," she panted and moaned as her hips slowly began to gyrate on their own.

"What can I do to make this better?" Scarface growled moving from Shekia's neck up to her earlobe.

"Eat this pussy," Shekia moaned. She could no longer control the fire that was growing in between her legs. "Eat this pussy," she repeated with more energy this time.

"That's what you want… Huh?" Scarface growled as he sped up his fingers forcing Shekia to cream in his hands.

"Yes baby, please"

"Are you begging me?"

"Yes baby, please eat this pussy. Please I want to cum in your mouth so bad baby. Please…," Shekia moaned. "I'm begging you, please…I need you."

Scarface quickly bent Shekia over in the closet, removed her soaking wet shorts, and slapped her ass. A moan escaped Shekia's lips as her ass jiggled from the slap.

"Spread your legs and grab your ankles!" Scarface demanded with authority. The tone he used with Shekia alone had her willing and ready to do any and everything he pleased.

Shekia stood wide legged and slowly bent over giving her man a show until she grabbed both of her ankles. Scarface melted down to his knees directly behind Shekia so he was face-to-face with her wet slightly hairy vagina. Scarface grabbed both of Shekia's ass cheeks, spread them apart, and stuck his tongue places a tongue wasn't supposed to go. He made sure he licked every inch of Shekia's peach, moving his tongue up and down quickly as if he was half man and half rattle snake. Immediately Shekia's clit became swollen, her legs tensed, and her breathing did the same.

"Oh my God," Shekia gasped. She couldn't take it no more. Scarface had forced her to cum for him again. Out of desperation, Shekia tried to move away from Scarface. Her clit was swollen and extremely sensitive, but Scarface could care less about her crying. He gripped Shekia's thighs locking her in place and sexually tortured her for trying to leave him. Scarface moved his tongue so fast that it felt like a vibrator instead of a tongue. Shekia arched her back and came a long drawn out orgasm. Scarface paused for a second or two making Shekia think that he was done. He waited for her body to relax a bit before he spread both of her ass cheeks apart and began eating her ass out.

"Oh my fucking God!" Shekia purred loudly. Greedy sounds came from her, sounds so primal that they scared her.

Twenty minutes later, Shekia was curled up in the bed sleeping like a baby. Scarface had fucked and sucked her the way she needed to be fucked and sucked and made her cum as if she had never come before. Whatever he did, the ending result was Shekia wasn't leaving; point blank period!

Scarface sat on the comfortable sofa that resided in their bedroom and watched Shekia sleep as he slowly sipped from his glass of vodka and cranberry juice. He knew that he hadn't heard the last of Mya and he would have to figure something out before she found a way to ruin him and Shekia's relationship. Scarface's cell phone buzzing snapped him out of his thoughts. He looked down and read the text that he had just received from his sister Vicky.

"Hey Scarface, thanks again for the money and the opportunity to put my acting skills to the test. I promise I won't let you down. I'll have that Bone guy wrapped around my finger in no time... WINK!"

Scarface smiled at the text message and then slid in the bed and joined Shekia.

Chapter 13

Capo entered the gym with Stacks and Hulk close on his heels. Several other guys who were affiliated with the Blood organization flanked behind the trio. Tonight was the start of the jails basketball tournament. Members from each dorm would play against inmates from other dorms. The teams would compete for a month and a half until there were only two teams remaining. The basketball tournament brought out each and every inmate. The entire gym was filled with inmates. There were several correctional officers lurking around the gym and others posted up. Their job was to keep the inmates in line and under control while the game was being played, but there were way too many inmates for the correctional officers to keep an eye on each and every one of them.

Capo, Stacks, and Hulk moved throughout the bleachers and took their seats amongst their peers. Other inmates may have showed up to the gym to watch the basketball game, but not

Capo. Capo was in the gym hoping to lay his eyes on Cash. The way Cash had humiliated Capo when he robbed him at the pool party was something that Capo wouldn't be able to let go, especially when the two men were locked up in the same jail.

The two men were bound to bump into one another sooner or later. Jail was a small place and word traveled fast behind the walls so Capo knew that more than likely word had already gotten back to Cash. The message was an unavoidable one. It was on site with them two and Capo was more than ready.

"This fuck nigga probably ain't even gone come out tonight," Stacks commented. He lived for action and drama. Every situation that presented itself, Stacks put himself dead smack in the middle no matter if it didn't even have anything to do with him. That's just how Stacks was.

"Fuck it! If he don't come out, then I'mma bring it to that nigga Wayne," Capo shrugged like it was no big deal.

Right on cue, Cash entered the gym with Wayne by his side. Immediately, Capo could tell that Cash had been getting his weight up. He remembered Cash being slimmer than he was now, but none of that mattered to him. All that mattered was there was nowhere for Cash to run, if he planned on running at all.

"Ain't that, that clown right there?" Hulk nodded in the direction of the two men entering the gym.

Capo nodded. "Yeah that's him." His palms instantly began to moisten as his adrenaline began to pump. Capo had been waiting for this day for so long that at this very moment it barely felt real.

"Fuck that! We bout to mob on these niggaz," Stacks huffed. He quickly turned to one of his flunkies and spoke. "Yo, go over there and tell that nigga Cash that Capo said to play the bathroom."

Capo, Stacks, and Hulk watched as the flunky got up and went to deliver the message.

* * * *

Cash and Wayne walked up the bleacher steps and found a seat in the middle of the aisle. Word had gotten back to Cash that Capo had just pulled up in the jail and was looking for him. After the way he had humiliated Capo, he knew that there was no way around the inevitable.

Cash was not the least bit worried. If it was one thing he knew how to do, it was fight. If all Capo wanted to do was fight, then he liked his chances, but he had to be real with himself. This was jail and it was no such thing as a fair fight anymore. Those days were long gone.

"Be on point," Wayne whispered over in Cash's ear. His eyes bounced from face-to-face looking for any signs of trouble. Wayne was from the old school and knew that this was the best time for shit to pop off. Besides Capo had already spread the word that when him and Cash bumped into each other, somebody was going to get knocked out. "You know Capo be with them fake ass Blood niggaz."

"I ain't worried about them," Cash said brushing it off.

"Well you should be," Wayne told him. "Them niggaz is like a million deep."

"Why you so worried about me for?" Cash asked. He didn't really trust Wayne, but he kept him close by because the man had a lot of connections that may come in handy one day in the near future.

"I feel like this is all my fault," Wayne explained. "If I had never hired you to rob Capo, you wouldn't be in the middle of this foolishness, and your partner Dough Boy would still be alive right now. I'm just saying…"

"Dough Boy wasn't my partner," Cash cut Wayne off. "He was family and if I didn't get locked up, he'd still be alive right now." That was another reason the beef between Cash and Capo couldn't be squashed or dead. Too much had happened for them to turn back now. The gloves were off and no punches were going to be held back.

"All I'm saying is that I feel like this is all my fault."

"Ain't nothing all your fault," Cash said quickly. "This the life we live. We both knew the rules to the game before we decided to play so it makes no sense to cry now." Cash was a street nigga to the fullest and beef was one of those things that when it came, you handled it and kept it moving. He wasn't a troublemaker, but he was a problem solver. "Besides this…"

A man that Cash and Wayne recognized as one of the Homies (Bloods) strolled up and interrupted the two's conversation. "Yo homeboy check this the fuck out," he spat looking at Cash. "Capo said to meet him in the bathroom in five minutes and don't blow it up either nigga."

"Fuck is you; the message boy?" Cash countered. "Matter fact, get out my face before I knock you the fuck out."

"What?" The messenger spat looking like he was ready to get it popping right there on the bleachers.

"You heard what the fuck he said!" Wayne barked. "If you want, you can play the bathroom too."

The messenger nodded his head up and down as he made a beeline straight for the bathroom.

Once the basketball game started and everyone's attention was focused on what was going on, on the court; Cash noticed Capo and two other men get up and smoothly and discreetly make their way to the bathroom.

Right at that moment Cash knew it was on and it was no turning back. He slowly stood up from his seat. Before he got a chance to take one-step, he felt Wayne grab his wrist.

"I'm coming with you," Wayne said.

"I'm good," Cash protested weakly. "I can handle this on my own."

Wayne shot Cash a disbelieving look. "Like I said, I'mma come with you." He looked over at two men who he rolled with and jerked his head signaling for them to follow him. The four men crept down from the bleachers and cautiously entered the death trap better known as the bathroom.

* * * *

Inside the bathroom, Capo stood awaiting the man who had successfully robbed him and gotten away with it. He was like a pit-bull waiting to be released from his leash.

Cash swiftly rounded the corner and immediately the two clashed toe-to-toe. Each man threw punches with bad intentions. Capo fired off a quick four-punch combination that he expected to slow Cash down, but instead Cash fought back just as hard and relentless. Each man did his best to inflict as much pain on the other as possible.

It was a violent and noisy fight. Both men tussled all over the bathroom. They crashed into the bathroom stall doors, collided with the sink and the unbreakable reflective Plexiglas, fought like animals, and didn't plan on stopping until only one man remained standing.

Cash threw a quick left hook followed by a straight hand that slipped through Capo's guard and left blood in his mouth. Tasting his own blood enraged Capo and caused him to lose his cool. He charged Cash throwing wild haymakers. He wanted to end the fight with one punch, a punch that was hard enough to knock out a horse.

Cash weaved the haymakers and landed a sharp uppercut to Capo's chin. The punch took Capo off his feet and caused him to bite his tongue. Once Capo hit the floor and Cash started getting the best of him, Wayne noticed the homies started inching their way closer and closer towards the action.

"Nah, nah back up playboy," Wayne warned the light skin cat with a head full of waves. "This one-on-one."

Without hesitation, Stacks turned and stole on Wayne. The punch sounded off loudly and sent Wayne stumbling back into the sink. Before Wayne got a chance to retaliate, he felt fist connect with his face and the side of his head coming from several different angles and directions. Wayne fought back as best he could, but when the big man joined in on the action, it was lights out.

Hulk's huge paw shot out and found a tight grip around Wayne's throat.

With all of his might, Hulk slammed the back of Wayne's head into the wall. A huge gash immediately opened up on the back of Wayne's head as his DNA began to spill out all over the floor.

Over in the corner Capo and Stacks stomped Cash out. Cash tried to fight them off for as long as he could, but the two on one battle quickly turned to a three on one. Cash balled up in the corner while hard kicks assaulted his rib cage. He silently prayed that the beating would stop, but he knew better. Capo wanted to kill him and wouldn't stop until the task at hand was completed.

Just when Cash felt like he was about to pass out from the beating he was taking, the sound of several correctional officers running up in the bathroom could be heard. Cash had never been happier to see the police in his life.

A big, white correctional officer ran up into the bathroom and struck Hulk in the back of his leg with his wooden nightstick. Hulk turned, looked at the correctional officer, and punched him in the mouth. The impact from the punch knocked the big white man out cold. Once the correctional officer went down, several correctional officers jumped on Hulk. Two correctional officers wrestled with Hulk trying to take him down while a few other correctional officers used their nightsticks as a sleeping pill and went upside Hulk's head.

Stacks and Capo quickly jumped into the brawl with the police when they saw Hulk being ganged up on. Police looked out for police and inmates looked out for inmates.

Seven minutes later the two crews had been separated and the correctional officers had the situation under control. Capo and Stack were taken straight to the box while Wayne, Cash, and Hulk were taken to the hospital. Their injuries didn't look too good and going to see the nurse wasn't going to cut it. They needed real medical attention.

After the brawl, Capo felt good about what he had accomplished. He had got some payback for what Cash had done to him, but most importantly, the word was sure to spread throughout the jail and make its way back to the streets.

Chapter 14

The cocaine-white 745 B.M.W. pulled into the designated club parking spot. The passenger door swung open and the voice of Young Jeezy banged through the car's speakers. Bone stepped out the passenger seat shining like a diamond. He wore his usual all-black. Around his neck hung three diamond studded chains and in his hand he held a Styrofoam cup with a pink substance inside.

Once Capo was out of the picture, Bone blew up. He took over all of Capo's old spots and stole all of his cliental. Even a few of Capo's old women switched sides and decided to join the winning team and right now Bone was winning. Bone knew that when Capo was released from jail the two had some unfinished business to take care of and he was cool with that. Capo had put Bone on and in the end, Bone had crossed him. The two men fought it out in the streets before Capo got locked up, but that wasn't good enough. Things were sure to escalate to the next level once Capo was released from prison.

The driver's door of the B.M.W. opened and out stepped Mike Murder. Mike Murder was the most ignorant and violent man known to mankind and he was Bone's new right hand man. Mike Murder wore his dreads pulled back in a ponytail that rested in the middle of his back. He too wore all black and held a Styrofoam cup in his hand. He wore an army dog tag around his neck. His wrists were covered in frozen water and he wore a ring on each finger on his left hand except for his thumb.

Bone and Mike Murder made the perfect combination. They stepped foot in the club and were assaulted by the stench of musk and a God-awful heat. Even with it being almost pitch black inside the club, the walls were still sweating.

Bone squeezed his way through the crowded club and headed straight for the bar. He bumped his way through the crowd, side stepping dancing couples, and stopping people from repeatedly stepping on his new high-top Prada sneakers. Bone reached the bar and ordered two bottles of Peach Cîroc. He kept one for himself and handed the other bottle to Mike Murder. Bone looked around and saw that he had several other goons in the club. His team seemed to be getting bigger and stronger with each passing day.

Bone thought about taking his talents to the V.I.P. area, but decided to stay near the dance floor since that was where the action was taking place. Not to mention that was where all the women were. Standing in front of Bone was a dark skin beauty. The woman wore a pair of white Good2Go leggings with red writing across the ass, white four-inch heels, and a white spandex fitting top that looked like it was suffocating her breast. The woman in all white had dreads that stopped a little below her shoulders.

Bone watched as the woman in all white bounce and shake her ass to the beat. From the way that the woman danced, if Bone had to guess he would say that she was from an exotic island of some sort.

The woman dressed in all white looked back and winked at Bone. She flashed a beautiful bright smile. Her hips and ass continued to move as if they had a mind of their own. Her ass moved like it was controlled by a remote control and the site alone brought a smirk to Bone's face.

He kept his eyes on the woman in all white's ass. Bone had to admit she was definitely looking like something and he was curious to see what shorty was about.

Jim Jones song "848" banged through the speakers and the club immediately went crazy. Gang members twisted their fingers, threw up gang signs, and repped their hoods while women sang along with Jim Jones word-for-word.

The woman in all white looked back at Bone and said, "Yeah it's real."

"Excuse me?" Bone said leaning down so he could hear the woman over the loud music.

"I said it's real," the woman in all-white said. "I saw you looking at my ass like I got some ass shots or something."

"I'll be the judge of that," Bone slurred as his hand rubbed all over the dark skin beauty's ass.

"Cut it out." She pushed him to a comfortable distance.

"You got a name?" Bone took a long swig from his bottle.

"Vicky"

"Yo, ma where you from?" Bone questioned as he analyzed the sexy woman that stood before him. He was used to having bad bitches so Vicky's looks didn't really impress him.

"Where I'm from?" Vicky echoed giving Bone a funny look. "What you a cop or something?"

Bone let out a soft chuckle. "Bitch don't ever disrespect the God like that again," he spat with his tone going from friendly to cold instantly. Usually Bone would have smacked the shit out of a bitch for coming at him like that, but tonight he was on some chill shit. Bone went to spin off, but Vicky quickly grabbed his wrist before he disappeared on her.

"Don't act like that." Vicky placed a friendly hand on Bone's chest in an attempt to get him to calm down. *"Come on Vicky...Don't fuck this up,"* she said to herself.

Vicky looked up in Bone's face and smiled. "I'm from Florida."

"Word?" Bone took another swig from his bottle. "Yeah you look like a Florida bitch."

Bone's disrespect caught Vicky off guard, but she remained calm. She figured she should just fight fire with fire. "You got a filthy mouth. Maybe I should put this pussy in it," she countered.

Her remark caused a smile to spread across Bone's face. He was used to chicks talking fly so Vicky's words didn't faze him one bit. "Do what you feel," was his response. For the rest of the night Bone ignored and only half listened to what Vicky was rambling about. His mind was on what was under Vicky's leggings. Bone wondered if Vicky's pussy was hairy or clean shaved. He wondered if listening to her ramble was worth what was in between her legs.

"You heard me?" Vicky's irritating voice brought Bone back to reality.

"Yeah," Bone answered looking down at the Rolex that decorated his wrist. "I'm saying though, it's getting late. You trying to do something or what?" He cut straight to the chase.

Bone's forwardness slightly offended Vicky. His arrogance was disgusting and a super turn off. Vicky couldn't wait until this assignment was over so she could head back to Miami and get back to her life. If this weren't so important to Scarface, Vicky would probably be in a hot tub somewhere enjoying the fruits of her labor.

"What you wanna grab a bite to eat or something?" Vicky suggested. She didn't know what else to say at the moment. From the way that Bone was looking at her, she could tell what was on his mind. She just hoped that Bone didn't see through her game.

Mike Murder quickly stepped in and whispered something in Bone's ear. Whatever Mike Murder had told, him caused Bone's face to crumble up. He nodded his head a few times while listening to his right-hand-man.

Vicky stood waiting to see what Bone wanted to do. She still couldn't believe that he had beat Shekia up as if she was a man. In her eyes that was some real sucker shit to do. He didn't get any points for beating up on a defenseless woman.

"I'm going to need a rain check," Bone said to Vicky and then pulled out his cell phone. "Let me get ya number real quick though and I'mma hit you up tomorrow or something."

"Is everything alright?" Vicky asked faking concern. Honestly, she could give two fucks if everything was all right with him or not. All she cared about was completing the mission at hand.

"Yeah, I'm good," Bone, replied quickly. "Just gotta go handle something real quick."

Vicky stored her number in Bone's phone, gave him a kiss on the cheek, and made him promise her that he was going to call her before allowing him to leave. As she watched Bone make his way towards the exit, she wondered what was so important that he had to leave so abruptly. Vicky jumped when she felt someone tap her on the shoulder. She quickly spun around and saw a nice looking heavyset man standing before her with his hips swaying back and forth to the Reggae tune that blasted through the speakers. The facial expressions that the heavyset man showed, told Vicky that he was really into the song and focused on his dance moves.

"Come on girl," the heavyset man yelled with a friendly smile on his face. His forehead was drenched in sweat. "You standing there like a statue. Come and dance with me."

"Nah I'm good," Vicky said with her eyes still on the path of Bone's exit. Before she had a chance to come up with her next move, the heavyset man grabbed Vicky's wrist and pulled her towards him. Before Vicky got a chance to protest, another ignorant drunk fool grabbed her waist from behind. The rest of the crowd got hype when they saw the two men lock Vicky in a sandwich.

Vicky fought and struggled to break away from the two sweaty drunk men, but it seemed like the more she struggled to free herself and break out of the sandwich, the more aggressive the men became with her. Just as Vicky got ready to scream, the sound of several loud thunderous shots rang out sending everyone in the club down to the floor. After a short pause, four more shots rang out sending the club into a frenzy.

Vicky scrambled towards the exit following the crowd. She didn't know what was going on, but deep down inside she knew that Bone had something to do with the shooting. All she could do now was wait and see if Bone would call her as he promised he would.

Chapter 15

Angela sat in an empty room with her hands cuffed behind her back. Her handcuffs were cuffed to the steel chair that she sat in, making it hard for her to move. She didn't have on anything but a bra and panties set. Angela didn't know what to expect from the authorities. Whatever they had planned for her, she didn't care. She just hoped that James' punishment wouldn't be too harsh. Inside Angela felt sorry for James. He didn't have a clue what he was getting himself into from the jump and now he had to suffer because of her. In the beginning, James' only crime was loving a beautiful woman. He had no clue who Angela really was and no clue that she was the enemy. Now for his lack of knowledge, he had to suffer.

Angela was trained and well prepared for whatever was to come. She just hoped it wouldn't be too bad.

Angela's face was covered in dried up blood and her wounds went unattended. The agents left Angela in solitary for hours. They wanted to mentally fuck her before the physical torture came into place.

An hour later, the door came busting open and in walked The Gladiator flanked by two men who wore suits with a bunch of pins and metals pinned down to their suit jacket's breast.

The Gladiator's combat boots sounded off loudly until they finally came to a stop right in front of Angela. After all the lies that were told to the media and press, The Gladiator was looking like some sort of hero. He looked down at Angela. He and she were the only two who really knew what had went down in the hotel room and inside he still felt a certain way.

"I swear to God you better start talking and you better start talking now!" The Gladiator barked looking down at Angela as if she was a child.

Angela looked up at The Gladiator unmoved and unfazed by his words. If they were waiting for Angela to talk, they were going to waiting for a very long time. She was trained not to talk and disciplined enough not to go against her training.

"You not going to talk?" The Gladiator growled.

Angela said nothing.

"Okay," The Gladiator said as he turned and punched Angela in her face. The force from the punch caused her head to violently snap back.

The Gladiator turned his gaze on the two men in the uniforms. "I think I'm going to need a little time alone with her," he said removing his hunting knife from down in its holster. The two agents smiled, and then gladly exited the room leaving The Gladiator and Angela alone.

"Now you listen to me and you listen to me carefully," The Gladiator began. The hunting knife in his hand glistened as if it had just been polished. "I'm going to ask you some very simple questions and I want some very simple answers."

Angela said nothing.

"Who the fuck is that other assassin in the suit? Do y'all two work together? Your best bet is to just tell me where I can find him because I'm just going to wind up finding him anyway."

Angela said nothing.

"You do know that the place that you're headed to is hell on earth, right?" The Gladiator paused for a second to let his words sink in. "You're going to be placed in a super max prison in a foreign country." He smiled. "Life in prison in America would be too easy, but life in prison in a foreign country is hell on earth and I promise you'll feel every single minute you spend in there or I could just kill you now," The Gladiator said. "Or you can just tell me what I need to know and then maybe we might be able to work something out…what do you say, huh?"

Angela said nothing.

"Who do you work for?"

Angela said nothing.

In a swift motion, The Gladiator brought the hunting knife down across Angela's chest. She yelled out in pain as a deep nasty gash opened up across her chest, her blood painting her feet as well as the floor red.

"Still don't want to talk?" The Gladiator smiled.

Angela said nothing, but her eyes spoke in volumes. She shot daggers at The Gladiator with her eyes. Her eyes told The Gladiator that if her hands weren't cuffed behind her back to the steel chair she sat in that she would kill him with her bare hands.

"Okay have it your way," The Gladiator said as he raised the hunting knife above his head, and then forcefully brought it down jamming the sharp point of the knife down in the center of Angela's thigh.

"ARRRGGHH!" Angela howled at the top of her lungs.

"You ain't so tough without your Teflon body armor," The Gladiator said taunting Angela. "Still don't want to talk?"

"Fuck you!" Angela growled. Her eyes showed no fear.

"Oh so you can talk." The Gladiator slowly circled Angela's chair. He was enjoying torturing Angela way more than he should have been. He didn't care what he had to do, but before he left that room, Angela was going to tell him what he wanted to know; even if he had to torture her to death... Literally!

"Who do you work for?" The Gladiator asked again.

"Fuck you!"

The Gladiator sighed loudly as he looked down at the hunting knife sticking out of Angela's thigh. At that point, he knew he couldn't use his hunting knife anymore out of fear of Angela losing too much blood so he came up with an even better idea. "I got something for ya ass," he barked and then stormed out of the room leaving Angela alone with nothing but her thoughts.

Angela looked down at the hunting knife sticking out of her thigh and did her best to block out the pain. She knew this was only the beginning to a long night. Her eyes glanced around the empty room repeatedly searching for a way out or something she could use to pick her handcuffs. Angela let out a defeated sigh as she came to the realization that it was no way out of the room. Her mind wondered what The Gladiator had in store for her. Whatever it was, Angela knew more than likely it would be painful. Seconds later the door came busting open and in walked The Gladiator. In one hand, he held a car battery and in his other hand, he held jumper cables. Another agent strolled in behind

The Gladiator carrying a small table. The agent set the table on its four legs, turned, and exited the room leaving The Gladiator and Angela alone.

The Gladiator sat the car battery on the table and clamped the jumper cables down to the battery while whistling a tuneless tune. He handled the jumper cables with care as if he was a seasoned mechanic.

"Still don't want to talk?" The Gladiator asked with his eyes focused on what he was doing. He didn't even have to look at Angela to see the fear in her eyes. He could only imagine what was going on in her mind.

"Fuck you!" was Angela's only reply. Her eyes glance down at the car battery, and then back up at The Gladiator. The smile that was etched across his face made her sick to her stomach.

"Okay! Have it your way," The Gladiator's voice boomed.

* * * *

In the next room, Agent James Carter sat in a steel chair and in front of him sat a cup of coffee and a pack of cigarettes. Across the table from him sat a red face agent who asked James the same questions one hundred different times in one hundred different ways. James took slow sips from his coffee when the sound of Angela screaming at the top of her lungs echoed through the thin walls. A hurt look flashed across James face and the fear of the unknown was evident.

"What are they doing to her over there?" James shot to his feet ready to defend and protect his woman.

"That's the least of your concerns," the agent said in a calm tone. "Have a seat please or else I'm going to be forced to restrain you," he warned. Another loud scream erupted from the other side of the wall causing James to think the worst.

"That's a female!" James growled through clenched teeth. "What y'all are doing is unnecessary!"

The agent looked at James and shook his head sadly. "She's a wanted assassin. What part of that don't you understand?"

"You don't understand…"

"No you don't understand!" The agent slammed his fist down on the table. "Your little girlfriend that you over here defending just killed several officers; hard working officers who left families behind so fuck you and your murdering girlfriend. The both of you can burn in hell for all I care!"

More screams could be heard coming from the room next door.

James went to respond, but a loud explosion erupted rattling the entire building. When James saw the shocked and nervous look on the agent's face, he grabbed his cup of coffee and splashed the hot liquid in the agent's face. Before the pain was even able to register, James grabbed the back of the agents head and violently slammed his face down into the table.

James swiftly fished through the unconscious agent's pockets until he came across a set of keys. He rushed over to the door, stepped out into the hall, and immediately smoke attacked his eyes and lungs. Agents scrambled by left and right looking for an emergency exit route. James spotted a small fire slowly spreading from he assumed the explosion had taken place.

James saw the room next door open and The Gladiator ran right pass him with his mind on the explosion and what had caused it.

James eased in the room and his heart leaped up to his throat at what his eyes saw. Angela sat cuffed to a steel chair with her head hung low. From where James stood, he couldn't tell if Angela was dead or just unconscious. Next to her sitting on a table was a car battery, and immediately James began to think the worst. He hurried over towards Angela, placed two fingers on her neck, and felt a weak pulse.

"You better not die on me," James said out loud. He used the keys he stole from the agent to remove the handcuffs from Angela's wrist. The sound of loud machine gun fire startled James and immediately he knew The White Shadow had arrived. James scooped Angela up in his arms as if a man would carry his new wife and exited the room in search of the closest exit.

Chapter 16

The White Shadow sat parked in an all-black luxury car across the street from the headquarters where Angela was being held. He was still pissed off with himself for letting Angela get away at the hotel. He was known for being a professional so all his moves replaying on the news didn't sit too well with him. Watching the hotel shooting on the news made The White Shadow feel like an amateur, but sometimes things didn't go according to plan. You had to take the good with the bad and not complain in the process.

As The White Shadow sat trying to figure out a way to get inside the F.B.I. headquarters, he spotted an agent exit the building heading to his unmarked vehicle. With the quickness of a cat, The White Shadow slipped out of his car with his 9mm with a silencer attached to the end of the barrel in his hand.

The agent reached his vehicle when a gloved hand covered his mouth and a gun was placed to the side of his head.

"Keep your mouth shut and come with me," The White Shadow demanded roughly escorting the agent over towards his luxury vehicle. The White Shadow reached down and removed the agent's wallet from his back pocket. "Get down on your knees," he barked as he began to fish through the agent's wallet. The White Shadow came across a few pictures of the agent's wife and two children. The White Shadow kept the business end of his gun trained on the agent as he popped the trunk and removed a heavy looking vest. "Here, put this on." He handed the vest to the agent.

"Wha... What's going on?" The agent stammered nervously. He recognized the man that stood over him as the man labeled as wanted on the news along with Angela.

"You're going to strap this bomb to your body and walk into the F.B.I.'s headquarters." The White Shadow explained to the agent, his tone was friendly and soft spoken.

"Never!" The agent spat looking up at The White Shadow as if he was the devil himself. "We don't negotiate with terrorist."

The White Shadow read the address that was on the agent's license out loud. "You do this for me and your family will be safe."

"And if I don't?" The agent asked, even though he already knew the answer to his question.

"You and your entire family will die and I'll make sure that your beautiful wife and lovely children won't be able to have an open casket," The White Shadow warned.

"Why? Why are you doing this?" The agent sobbed. "What kind of monster are you?"

"I'm America's worst nightmare," The White Shadow replied seriously. "Now what's it going to be?"

The agent sat silent for a few seconds as if he was in deep thought trying to weigh his options. "Tell my wife and children that I love them," was the agent's response.

The White Shadow nodded his head, removed a small remote control sensor from his pocket, and said "Will do soldier." He tapped a button on the remote and instantly a few lights lit up on the vest that was now attached to the agent's body.

"You know you're never going to get away with this, right?" The agent said trying to convince himself more than the assassin that played God with his life.

"Yeah I know," The White Shadow said sarcastically.

"I'll see you in hell!" The agent growled through clenched teeth as he turned and headed across the street in the direction of the building where Angela was being held captive.

The White Shadow waited until the agent was fully inside the building before he pushed down on a button on the remote and watched the front of the building explode and erupt in flames. The White Shadow popped his trunk and removed two Tech-9s, and then smoothly walked across the street and entered the headquarters building.

The White Shadow fired at anything he saw moving as he stepped through the building as if he owned the place. He watched as agents scrambled for their pathetic lives. The agents were like sitting ducks and this was nothing but target practice for The White Shadow. He dropped two agents who were brave enough to try and stand their ground. The Tech-9s fired loudly. The first agent suffered from a quick shot to the head and the body of the man standing to his left got riddled with hot bullets. Both men toppled face down onto the tiled floor and their souls evicted from their bodies before they could even count to one.

Out of nowhere, a muscular white man sprung from behind a wall and fired off a quick series of shots. One of the shots hit The White Shadow in his ribs causing his body to buckle. The shot hurt him, but it didn't drop him. The Gladiator fired off a few rounds from his handgun then quickly took cover behind the wall. The shot didn't penetrate through The White Shadow's bulletproof clothing, but from experience he could tell that his ribs had been cracked or either fractured. The White Shadow quickly returned fire with the Tech-9's rattling in each hand as bullets decorated the walls, vending machines, and small offices.

The Gladiator sprung from behind the wall, fired off a few more rounds, and then tried to dash in the office closest to him. Several Tech-9 bullets ripped and tore through The Gladiator's body. The impact from the shots added with his momentum caused his body to windmill through the air before crashing violently down to the floor.

The White Shadow smoothly released the spent clips from the base of his guns and replaced them with fresh ones. He walked over to The Gladiator, stood over his body, and then riddled his body with more bullets. The Gladiator's dead body shook like a ragdoll as bullets pumped through his body. The White Shadow stepped over The Gladiator's body and continued on throughout the building in search of The Teflon Queen.

* * * *

James carried Angela in his arms as he hurried throughout the building in search of an exit. At first, Angela's body weight didn't affect James, but the longer he carried her, the more his arms felt like they were on fire and about to fall off. James barged inside a small office as the loud sound of gunfire continued to ring out. Inside the office, James saw a small window. "That shit gone have to make due," he said to himself. He gently laid Angela down on the floor. Once Angela's half-naked body touched the cold floor she began to stir. James walked over toward the glass, cocked his arm back, and fired a sharp elbow at the center of the window. Seconds later, the sound of glass shattering could be heard.

"Baby?" Angela sat up. Her voice was groggy and dry. "Where am I?"

"Not now baby," James told her as he helped her up to her feet. "We have to go."

"Where's my clothes?" She asked confused. More gunfire followed by loud screams could be heard throughout the building. The sound of gunfire brought Angela back to her senses real quick. Immediately, she whispered, "He's here; The White Shadow."

James helped Angela out of the window first. She had saved his life so many times, so it was only right that he return the favor. He quickly squeezed out the small window and landed awkwardly down in the grass. He helped Angela up to her feet as the two moved through the grass at a not so quick pace. Angela not being a hundred percent made it hard to move at top speed. She hobbled like a wounded animal, but she was determined to stay alive. Grass turned into hard concrete when they reached the parking lot.

"Which car you wanna grab?" James asked sucking in as much air as his lungs could take.

"Don't matter," Angela said as the sound of gunfire erupted behind them and bullets pinged and ponged off the body of the car closest to them. Angela and James ran in a low crouching position until they reached an all-black Sedan. James sent his fist through the driver side window and then let himself inside. He hit the unlock-all button on the panel and watched Angela slide into the backseat through the rearview mirror. James pulled down the visor and the keys to the Sedan dropped down into his lap.

"Bingo!" James started the car, threw the Sedan in drive, and sped out the parking lot like a mad man. "You alright back there?"

"Yeah, I'm fine," Angela, replied. She stared out the window and watched light poles fly pass in a blur. "Slow down and do the speed limit so we don't attract unwanted attention."

"Where do we go from here?" James asked with his eyes focused on the road.

"I have a safe house that no one knows about out in the Poconos."

"Where, in Pennsylvania?" James asked.

"Yeah," Angela answered quickly.

"And you sure don't nobody know about this so-called safe house?" James was just beginning to trust Angela again, but he just had to make sure that she was sure about this safe house. The whole point of a safe house was that it was supposed to be safe.

"Positive baby." Angela climbed into the front seat and winced in pain. Immediately, James eyes diverted from the road down to the gaping hole that sat in the center of Angela's thigh. Just by looking at her face, James could tell that she was in severe pain.

"You alright?"

"Yeah, I'll be fine," Angela, said waving the deep gash in her thigh off. "I have a First-Aid kit and medical supplies over at the safe house," Angela told him. She thought it was cute that James was concerned about her. "Thank you."

"For what?"

"For saving me back there," Angela, said smiling weakly. She was happy to be alive, but on the inside, she felt like shit.

James chuckled. "If I save you around four more times, then we will be even."

For the rest of the ride James and Angela rode in silence, each caught up in their own thoughts. Silently, James wondered just how long it would be before The White Shadow tracked them down and popped up at the safe house. He respected Angela's skills and felt safe when in her presence. She may have been a dangerous and deadly assassin, but whatever she was, she was now his. James was tired of denying how he really felt about Angela. She had proved herself to be loyal and trust worthy, and honestly all the shooting and killing made James love Angela even more. It was something about a woman who knew how to use a gun that turned him on. "I love you."

Angela glanced over at James with a surprised smile on her face. "Where did that come from?"

"Don't worry about all that," he said jokingly. "Just know that I love you."

"I know you do."

"How do you know?" James asked curiously.

"I just know," Angela, said smiling. "Turn left right here. Go all the way down to the end of the street and it's the only house at the top of the hill."

The Sedan's tires crunched through fresh snow as it navigated them to their final destination. James pulled up in front of the safe house and Angela quickly hopped out in the freezing cold. She punched a code in the keypad on the side of the house and seconds later, the garage door slowly began to rise. Then hopped back in the passenger seat and James quickly pulled the Sedan into the garage.

The first thing Angela did when they stepped foot inside the safe house was tend to her wounds. Meanwhile, James strolled through the "safe house" that favored a mini mansion in complete awe. He never dated a woman for what she had or how much money she made, but from the looks of things, Angela seemed to be rolling in dough. This only meant she must have killed a lot of people, but none of that mattered to James because he was already in too deep.

"What do you think of the place?" Angela asked while stitching herself up.

"I think it's huge," James replied. "I bet you come out here all the time to get a peace of mind."

"Actually this is only my second time ever stepping foot in this place," she said honestly, as she peeked at the surveillance monitors that rested on the counter. Angela opened a packet of B.C. powder and took it dry to help with her pain. "You like it?"

"I love it," James said. "But I love you more."

"Do you really?" Angela hopped down off the counter and limped over towards James. She walked stiffly as though every step was killing her.

"I promise you I do," he said looking her dead in her eyes.

"You love me enough to run me some bath water and then scrub my body from head to toe?" Angela purred.

James glanced down at Angela's dirty and bloody feet. "I don't know about all that." He laughed. "How about I wash you from head to ankle?"

Angela looked down at her dirty toes and couldn't do anything but laugh. She was all beat up and needed time for her body to get repaired. Even The Teflon Queen needed time for her wounds to heal. People who had to go up against her may have thought she was invincible, but the truth was she was a mere mortal just like everyone else. "I got a few cuts and bruises so now you don't love me no more?" Angela kissed James on the lips. "Is that what it is?"

"It's going to take a lot more than a few cuts and bruises to stop me from loving you," James said strongly. He swiftly scooped Angela up in his arms and carried her upstairs to the bathroom where he ran Angela a nice hot bubble bath. Angela winced as she eased down into the hot water.

"Aww," Angela exhaled. The hot water was just what her body needed. Her body was beat up and sore from all the shit she had been through. She was happy to be alive and even happier that she was able to keep James alive through all of this. "Thank you."

"You are more than welcome," James said. He sat on the edge of the hot tub with a sponge in his hand. "It ain't no turning back for me now." He chuckled.

"If you want, I promise you can stay here forever," Angela told him. "The house is already paid for, there are two brand new cars in the garage, I have $500,000 in the safe downstairs, and you can have it all." Angela knew that James entire world had been turned upside down thanks to her. She also knew that it was no way that he would be able to go back to living a normal life even if he wanted to.

"How did you get into this business?" James asked. He gently lifted one of Angela's feet into his hands and began to wash it.

"My mother was killed right in front of me when I was five years old." Angela spoke with her eyes closed. James could tell that whatever she was about to tell him was something she had kept caged in for years. "I never forgot what my mother's killer looked like. I told an old police officer what I saw," Angela paused. "I also told him that when I got older I would murder my mother's killer. Long story short, this old man took me in and come to find out, he had been in the military for years, and once upon a time he used to be a sharp-shooter."

James listened intensively to every word that Angela spoke while he continued to wash her body.

"We followed my mother's killer for months. We watched him, learned his patterns, learned his habits, studied him, and studied him to the point where we knew what his next move would be before he even made it," Angela said. "In the meantime, the old man taught me everything there was to know about guns. He trained and taught me how to kill for two years until he felt I was finally ready for action... When the day finally came, I laid flat on my stomach on the roof with a sniper rifle in my hands. The old man laid right next to me and didn't say a word. He had been training me for two years so there was nothing left for him to say. I looked through my scope until my mother's killer finally showed his face. One head shot and he was gone."

"So your first kill was when you were seven years old?" James asked just wanting to be sure that the two were on the same page. He could only imagine what it could have been like to see his mother get murdered right before his eyes. That had to be traumatizing for any child.

Angela nodded her head. "After that, the old man continued to train me and when I turned sixteen he introduced me to a man named Mr. Biggz and the rest is history. I've been a contract killer ever since."

"Whatever happened to the old man?" James asked curiously.

"There was this top notch assassin from Russia," Angela began. "Mr. Biggz wanted me to team up with this assassin and form some kind of super assassin team, but I turned down his offer so Mr. Biggz went to the old man and tried to get him to convince me to team up with this young well known Russian assassin. The old man told Mr. Biggz that I was my own woman and that he had to respect my decision. Two weeks later, I found the old man dead in his living room," she explained as her eyes began to get watery. "I suspected that Mr. Biggz had hired the Russian assassin to murder the old man, but there was no way I could prove it."

"The young Russian assassin that Mr. Biggz wanted you to team up with was The White Shadow, wasn't it?" James asked.

Angela nodded as a few tears escaped her eyes and slowly rolled down her cheeks. "Ever since then, The White Shadow turned even more ruthless with his contracts earning him the reputation of the most vicious and number one assassin in the world."

"Open your legs," James ordered as he took a wash rag and thoroughly cleaned between Angela's legs. He made sure he moved his hand gently and delicately until he was sure that, her vagina was clean.

"So now that Mr. Biggz put a contract out on me, The White Shadow has a lot to prove."

"Teach me."

"Huh?"

"Teach me," James repeated.

"Teach you what?"

"Teach me what the old man taught you," James said.

"You ain't ready for that," Angela countered. She wouldn't be able to live with herself if something happened to James on the strength of her. This life wasn't for him. He wasn't built for this type of danger and pain that was sure to come and Angela wasn't sure if he had the heart to kill a police officer or a woman if he had to. In a split second, would he be able to pull the trigger or would he freeze up?"

"I'm not letting you go up against The White Shadow alone so you might as well teach me everything you know… We a team now," James said smiling. "Two killers are always better than one."

"I'm not sure if you are ready for all that," Angela said reluctantly. "I would have to teach you how to fight, how to drive, how to shoot, and how to turn anything in site into a weapon… This is hard work. It is more mental than physical… You sure you ready for this?"

James nodded his head. "Once my training is complete, me and you can be that super assassin team that you was telling me about," he said smiling. "We can call ourselves…" He paused for a second. "I don't know. We can figure all that out later, but yes I want you to teach me and I'm a fast learner."

"Once all of my wounds heal, training will begin," Angela said in a low whisper. She still wasn't sure if this was a good idea or not, but at the moment she didn't have a lot of options to choose from. "I'm telling you while I'm training you; I'm not your girlfriend. This training won't be easy at all. When it's all said and done, you probably won't even like me no more," she told him.

"Good!" James smiled. "Cause I already don't like you... I love you!"

Chapter 17

Vicky sat in her hotel room texting one of her home girls. The trip to New York wasn't turning out as she planned. Nothing seemed to be going her way. She badly wanted to return back to Miami, but she had promised Scarface that she would help him out with the situation. Besides, she had already spent half of the money that Scarface had paid her for her services.

Vicky sat trying to come up with a plan on how she could speed up the process on getting rid of Bone. A sharp knock at the door startled Vicky. She wasn't expecting anyone, especially at this time of night. Vicky swiftly hopped up off the bed when the knock returned again, but this time a little louder and with more determination than the first knock. Vicky stood in a pair of boy shorts, a matching bra, and her hair was wrapped up in a scarf because she had no plans of going back out for the night. Vicky snatched a white cotton robe from behind the bathroom door and quickly covered herself. Then she made her way over to the door to see who in the hell was disturbing her at this time of night.

Vicky looked through the peephole, and on the other side of the door stood Bone and his right hand man Mike Murder. Once Vicky cracked open the door, Bone and Mike Murder swiftly barged inside the hotel room not bothering to wait for an invitation. "Get dressed," Bone ordered. The seriousness in his eyes made Vicky nervous. Had her cover been blown? Were they there to kill her? Did they somehow find out that Scarface was her brother? A million thoughts ran through Vicky's mind.

"Is everything alright?" She asked trying to buy herself a few seconds to come up with her next move.

"Bitch I said get dressed!" Bone barked. On his command, Mike Murder removed a gun from his waistband. His body language told Vicky that if she tried to procrastinate for one second longer he would blow her head off of her shoulders. Vicky quickly threw on a pair of jeans, a thin sweater, snatched her scarf off of her head, and pulled her hair back into a loose raggedy ponytail.

"Can you tell me what this is all about now?" Vicky asked with her hands glued to her hips.

From the look on Bone's face, she could tell that he had been drinking.

"You talk too fucking much," Bone snarled. His tone showed no respect what so ever and that pissed Vicky off. Mike Murder grabbed Vicky by the arm and led her out of the room.

Downstairs an all-black GMC truck sat awaiting curbside. Mike Murder hopped up in the passenger seat while Bone and Vicky slid in the back seat. On Vicky's face, it looked as if she had an attitude, but on the inside, she was scared to death. She had no clue what lay ahead and all she could do was pray for the best. Vicky sat in the back seat watching Bone carefully. In his hand, he held a thin, clear plastic cup that held a dark brown liquid, which Vicky assumed, was Hennessy.

"Can I have some?" Vicky said nodding down towards Bone's cup.

Bone's hand moved in a blur as he splashed the substance that was inside the cup in Vicky's face. "You want some more?"

Vicky wiped her face clean as best she could with her hands. At that moment, Vicky knew she was as good as dead. It made no sense to try and think positive. She had saw the aftermath up close and in person at what Bone had done to Shekia and she hadn't even done anything to him so she could only imagine what he had in store for her. Vicky decided to just keep her mouth shut and see what was to come next. The truck was pulling over now. The speed dropped and the ride went from a smooth highway type of ride to driving on what she figured to be rocks and gravel.

The truck came to a complete stop out in the middle of nowhere. Vicky glanced out the dark tinted window and noticed a rundown looking building that had seen its better days. She silently wondered if this would be the place where she would take her last breath. The back door opened and Mike Murder roughly snatched Vicky out of the back seat. Her feet hit the uneven pavement so hard that her ankle almost snapped.

"Damn, my nigga!" Vicky huffed trying to jerk her arm free from Mike Murder's grip. Mike Murder forced Vicky through the front door of the raggedy looking house. Vicky was about to curse Mike Murder and Bone the fuck out, but all the mean faces that sat posted up in the living room staring back at her caused fear to creep up in her heart and that fear made her keep her mouth shut.

Once Bone entered the house, he dramatically slammed the door behind him causing everyone in the living room to give him their undivided attention. Bone took a slow sip from his cup while looking at Vicky the whole time. "You a cop?"

"Huh?"

"Bitch you heard him!" Mike Murder called from the sideline.

"A cop?" Vicky echoed. "Never! That's what this is all about?"

Bone looked over at Mike Murder and gave him a simple head nod. In a flash, Mike Murder turned and stole on the man standing next to him. The punch dropped the scrawny man, but it didn't put him out.

"Yo! What the fuck?" The scrawny man said slowly climbing back to his feet holding his jaw with a confused look on his face.

"We got a rat in our organization!" Bone sipped his drink slowly and then frowned. "You two are the newest recruits... Everything has been quiet up until now which leads me to believe that one of you is the rat!"

"It's her!" The scrawny man said quickly pointing the finger at Vicky in an attempt to get the heat and pressure off of him. "This bitch looks like a cop," he accused.

"Nigga you can't be serious!" Vicky looked at the scrawny man and shook her head sadly.

"I know how we can get down to the bottom of this," Bone said in a smooth slur. "Both of you motherfuckers strip!"

"Huh?" The scrawny man said as he immediately broke out into a cold sweat. "Come on Bone? You know I ain't no snitch," he protested. "Who is this bitch? I mean where did she even come from?"

All eyes in the room shifted to Vicky for a response. Vicky didn't reply. Instead, she began to strip down to her birthday suit. She wasn't a cop so she had nothing to worry about. Her biggest fear was Bone finding out that Scarface was her brother. Once she figured out that, that wasn't what Bone had brought her down to the raggedy house for, she breathed a sigh of relief. Vicky stood in the middle of the living room completely in the nude. She raised her arms out to her side and moved around in a circle letting everyone in the living room see that she wasn't wearing a wire. "You happy?"

Bone gave her a head nod. "Put your clothes back on."

By now, all eyes were locked and glued to the scrawny man who stood in the middle of the living room still fully dressed.

"I don't have all day," Bone said with a raised brow.

"Come on Bone… It's a house full of men in here. That's some gay shit." The scrawny man announced trying to weasel his way out of the sticky situation he found himself in the middle of.

"Motherfucker I said strip!" Bone barked. The look in his eyes told the scrawny man that he had two choices. He either could strip or get clapped. One of Bone's goons eased up on the scrawny kid from behind, covered his mouth with his hand, and placed a sharp knife to his throat.

Right on cue, Mike Murder walked up to the scrawny man and lifted up his shirt. Taped to his chest was a small microphone. The look on his face was the look of a man who had just got caught masturbating by his grandmother. Immediately, Mike Murder removed the scrawny man's wallet from his back pocket and tossed it to a few young knuckleheads that were dying to get their name up in the streets. The two young knuckleheads removed the man's I.D. and then made a beeline for the door. The cops were listening on the wiretap so there was no way Bone and his crew would be able to get away with killing the scrawny man, but the two young knuckleheads were headed to the scrawny man's home address to pay his family a visit.

Bone quickly grabbed Vicky by the hand and led her back to the truck that awaited them outside. Once they got in the back seat, it was clear that Vicky had an attitude. Her arms were folded across her chest, a mean scowl on her face, and for some reason she couldn't get one of her legs to stop shaking and stay still. It just seemed to move on its own with a nervous bounce.

Bone placed a gentle hand on Vicky's thigh only for her to slap it away.

"Don't you dare touch me?" She growled. She was on fire and couldn't believe she had let Bone humiliate her back there the way he did. If her brother found out what Bone had done to her, he would be sleeping with the fish somewhere. *"Matter of fact, that's exactly what I'm going to do. I'm going to tell Scarface about what just happened as soon as I get back to my room,"* Vicky said to herself.

"Come on Mami, don't act like that," Bone said sipping from his cup. "I'd rather be safe than sorry."

"Well I'm glad to know that your safety means everything to you," Vicky huffed with an attitude. She wanted nothing else to do with Bone. She was even willing to give Scarface his money back. If Vicky would have knew that she would have to go through all this just to earn Bone's trust, she would have never agreed to the job.

"You still mad?" Bone asked as if a few hours had passed and not a few seconds.

"What you mean am I still mad?" Vicky huffed. "You damn right I'm still mad! You just made me strip down in front of a room full of strangers!"

"How long you gone be mad for?" Bone asked nonchalantly.

"Just don't say anything else to me for the rest of the night," Vicky said rolling her eyes. The sooner she could get away from Bone, the better. She hadn't even known him that long and already she couldn't stand him. If Bone stepped out of the truck and got hit by a bus, Vicky wouldn't lose an ounce of sleep.

The truck slowed to a stop right in front of the hotel that Vicky was staying at. Juelz Santana's mix tape *"God Will'n"* bumped through the speakers as the driver hit the hazards. Bone glanced down at his watch and then over at Vicky. "You still mad?" He asked as if something had changed.

"Good night Bone," Vicky spat, hopped out of the truck, and entered the hotel. If she had a gun in her possession at the moment, nine times out of ten she would have left Bone's brains all over the truck's interior. Vicky made it inside of her room, stripped down, and headed straight for the shower. She felt filthy on the inside, degraded, and she still couldn't believe Bone had the audacity to make her strip in front of a room full of strangers. At the end of the day, he had to know that she wasn't the police. No matter how hard Vicky scrubbed her skin she still felt dirty, like she had been rolling around in the dirt all night. Vicky didn't know how she would break the news to Scarface explaining to him that she could no longer help him out with this Bone thing. It was just too much, way too much.

Vicky stepped out the shower and slipped on a cotton robe. She walked throughout her room barefoot. She bent down a removed a bottle of wine from the mini fridge, popped the cork with a small corkscrew, grabbed a glass from off the counter, and then sat it back down. Fuck a glass! She raised the bottle up to her lips and took it straight to the head. Taking small sips would do her no good at a time like this. Vicky raised the bottle up to her lips again, but paused at the sound of a sharp knock at her hotel room door.

"Now what?" Vicky said to herself wondering who was disturbing her now. After the type of day she had, all Vicky wanted was to be left alone.

Vicky opened the door and saw Bone standing on the other side. "What do you want now?" She asked in a tone that let Bone know that she was fed up with him. Bone let himself inside Vicky's room and shut the door behind him. In a swift motion, he snatched open Vicky's robe, pressed his body up against hers, turned his head to an angle, and kissed Vicky as if he had just recited he words, *"I do."*

For a second, thoughts of cracking Bone upside his head with the wine bottle crossed Vicky's mind, but for some reason she kissed him back. She kissed him as if she had been patiently waiting years for this moment. She started to get damp and moist in between her legs. Before Vicky knew it, the wine bottle had dropped down to the floor and her arms locked around Bone's neck.

Bone pulled away from Vicky, took a step back, and looked in her eyes. Her eyes told Bone that she was on fire and she was in a bad need of an orgasm. "Get down on your knees and suck this dick!" He demanded. The charge and authority in his voice only turned Vicky on even more. Vicky quickly got down on her knees like a good girl and began to suck the shit out of Bone's dick.

Vicky abandoned her lady like ways, her politeness, and became sexual and primal as her head moved at a steady experienced rhythm. She could feel Bone's hands in her hair helping to guide her head the perfect speed.

"This what you wanted; right?" Bone asked feeding Vicky dick. "You like sucking on this dick; don't you?"

"Mmm…hmmm," she moaned in between slurps.

"I can't hear you!" Bone barked as he began to fuck Vicky's mouth even faster and with more force. His length was causing her to gag every so often.

"Mmmmm…hmmmm!" Vicky moaned loudly. She squeezed Bone's ass, wanting him to feed her his dick. She welcomed his aggression and fury. Vicky's moans told Bone that she wanted more. Bone was going so deep down Vicky's throat that she could feel his balls slapping against her chin with each stroke.

"You want me to cum in your mouth?" Bone spat looking down at Vicky.

"Mmm…hmm," Vicky moaned. When she felt Bone's dick began to swell, she bobbed her head even faster and sucked harder until Bone exploded in her mouth. Vicky moaned long and good as she swallowed everything like a big girl.

She looked up at Bone's still erect penis while attempting to catch her breath. The way Bone fucked Vicky's mouth made her horny and had her pussy soaking wet and on fire. "Fuck me," Vicky said in a sexually charged voice. She was still on her knees looking up at Bone as if he was God Almighty. "Fuck me," she said again. This time she spoke in a more demanding tone.

"That's what you want?" Bone asked stepping out of his jeans. Then he removed his shirt and looked down into Vicky's pleading eyes as she nodded her head up and down. Bone took Vicky right there in the middle of the floor, missionary style, face to face, and tongue to tongue. Bone sank deep. He came out and sank deep again while kissing Vicky in the process. Each kiss was more intense than the last one. Each kiss was desperate and loud and each stroke was devastating.

"Yes," Vicky moaned with her eyes shut tight. "Beat this pussy up!" Her frown deepened and became the most beautiful ugly face Bone had ever seen.

The sounds that escaped Vicky's lips along with the faces she made only excited Bone even more. Then Bone started making an ugly face, straining, and pumping hard like a mad man. Vicky's hands were forcing him deeper into her wetness, encouraging him to reach satisfaction

A few pumps later, Bone let out a loud groan. His body went stiff and then collapsed down on top of Vicky. He got up and quickly got himself together. He looked down at Vicky's body sprawled out across the floor as she had just been thrown out of a fourth floor window. "You alright?"

"Oh my God," was all Vicky said.

Bone smiled and said, "I'll call you tomorrow." Then he made an exit leaving Vicky in the middle of the floor in a whole other world.

Chapter 18

Scarface sat in a beach chair over by the side of the pool while he watched Shekia swim freely like a fish. A pair of Ray Bans covered his eyes as he sipped on a strong drink. He didn't have the heart to tell Shekia that he had been silently paying Mya to stay away from her. Ever since Mya's first unexpected visit, she had threatened to do harm to Shekia if her demands were not met. At first Scarface was going to tell Mya to go fuck herself, but the more he thought about it, the more he realized that Mya did indeed have enough power and influence to ruin him and Shekia's relationship if she really wanted to.

Scarface didn't want any trouble so he agreed to pay Mya a couple of dollars to stay as far away from him and Shekia as possible. Water splashing on Scarface's feet and legs snapped him out of his thoughts. He looked down and saw Shekia in the water resting her arms on the edge of the pool with a bright pretty smile on her face. "Come get in the water with me," she sang. "I know you ain't too good to get wet." She splashed Scarface's feet.

"I'm having a good time watching you enjoy yourself," Scarface said. "Plus I don't really do chlorine water. It makes my joint look small." He nodded down towards his crotch area.

"Ain't nobody out here but me and you? Besides I know how big that Jimmy is," Shekia said licking her lips as thoughts of the sex session her and Scarface had last night popped inside her head.

"Maybe later baby," Scarface said. His phone made a pinging sound letting him know that someone had texted him. Before he could look down at his phone, it pinged again letting him know another text message had popped up.

"You ain't no fun," Shekia said waving him off. She hopped on a yellow blow up raft and slowly floated away.

Scarface looked down at his phone and read the first text message that was from his sister Vicky. *"Hey big head... Sorry but this mission is a little more complicated than expected, but you know lil sis gon come through for you like always... This shouldn't take no longer than a few more days. I got you. Luv ya!"*

Scarface shook his head and smiled. Vicky was a trip, but she was family and he knew if anybody could get this job done, it was she. He scrolled down to his next text message and saw that it was from Mya. Instantly the smile that was just on his face flipped upside down. *"Fuck this bitch want,"* he said to himself as he read the text message.

Mya: *Come over to my house. I need to talk to you about something... And yes, it is important.*

Scarface: *Nah, I'm doing something right now. I'll get up with you another time.*

Mya: *Nigga please! You probably aren't doing shit right now. Stop playing with me!*

Scarface: *Listen I don't have time for your childish games right now. Like I said, I'm busy right now and I'll get up with you another time.*

Mya: *Nigga I need to talk to you about something right now. I said it's important, now you can come over here, or I can come over there and trust me you don't want me coming over there! Don't try me!*

Scarface: *If it's so important then why can't you call me right now so we can talk?*

Mya: *Nah this a conversation that we need to have face to face.*

Mya: *Be here within the next hour or else I'm coming over there.*

Scarface: *OMW* (on my way)

Scarface cursed Mya out in his mind. She knew just how to piss him off, and what buttons to push to get a reaction out of him. Mya had Scarface by the balls and she knew it.

"Baby, I gotta make a run real quick. I'll be back in a little while." Scarface made a circle with his hands and put them up to his mouth so his voice could travel and reach Shekia out in the pool.

"Okay baby and be careful. I love you!" Shekia yelled with a smile and then blew Scarface a kiss. Scarface opened up his hand and then crossed it signaling that he had caught the kiss she had blown his way.

Chapter 19

Scarface pulled his grey B.M.W. into Mya's driveway and killed the engine. The first thing he noticed was Mya had her front door open. The screen door made it hard for Scarface to see inside, but he knew she left the front door open so that she could see when he pulled up.

Scarface slid out the B.M.W. and smoothly bopped over towards the front door. Before he could raise his fist to knock on the screen door, it flew open.

"You got here just in time," Mya huffed. "I was getting ready to get dressed, head over to your crib, and raise hell."

Scarface followed Mya inside the house. He did his best not to strangle her right there at the door. Mya had a stank, sexy, my ass is too big for my body type of walk. Scarface hated her walk, but for some reason he couldn't keep his eyes off of her when she walked. Mya wore a pair of red booty shorts that revealed half of her ass, some rainbow colored socks that came up to her knees, a white wife beater, and her hair sat up on the top of her head in a loose bun.

"What's so important that I had to come all the way across town," Scarface asked. "And I swear to God whatever it is, it better be a life or death emergency!"

"You thought about what we talked about?" Mya asked with her arms folded.

"What are you talking about?"

"Us being a family," Mya said refreshing his memory.

Instantly Scarface's nose began to flare as fire could be seen dancing in his eyes. "You made me come all the way over here for that?" He asked with his face crumbled up. At that very moment, he wanted to punch Mya in her face for wasting his time just because she could.

Mya caught an attitude as if she was the one who had just driven across town for some bullshit. "So what you saying? Our family ain't important?"

"What family?"

"I told you that I been thinking about starting a family," Mya snarled.

"With who?" Scarface asked. Mya had to know that there was no way he was going to impregnate her with his seed. Never in a million years would he ever go that route with her. She was a drama queen and she didn't care about anyone but herself.

"With who?" Mya repeated looking Scarface up and down, giving him the evil eye. "You wanna play? Cause we can play if that's what you want," she said with her voice rising with each word she spoke.

"Listen," Scarface began. "I and you are not family. We never will be, and I definitely don't' want to start a family with you, Mya. I have a girlfriend."

"But she ain't me," Mya blurted out.

"I don't want you!" Scarface yelled letting his anger get the best of him. "What part of that don't you understand?"

"Well fuck you then!" She said as if continuing the conversation would stop her from doing something more important.

"Now what?" Scarface asked. He was still pissed that he had driven all the way across town for this bullshit. He could have been doing so many other important things rather than going back and forth with his ex.

"Now you can get the fuck out," Mya countered slyly. Scarface had made her feel low, stupid, as apiece of garbage, but little did he know he had just made a big mistake. Scarface shook his head as he headed for the door, but Mya's voice caused him to stop dead in his tracks.

"Tell your little girlfriend Shekia she better watch her back," Mya yelled with a smirk on her face. She knew her words would cut Scarface deep. Mad that her little plan didn't work, Mya was willing to do anything to make Scarface's life miserable.

"Mya I'mma tell you this one time and one time only..." The sound of turning keys and the front door opening then slamming hard caused Scarface to abandon what he was saying and look over towards the door. Standing in front of the door was a big brolic dark skin man whose muscles were so big that they looked fake. If Scarface had to guess, the dark skin man had to stand between 6'7 and 6'8 rock solid. In the man's hands were bags filled with groceries.

"Who the fuck is this nigga?" The giant asked Mya, sitting grocery bags on the floor with a clank.

Scarface and Mya exchanged glances. Mya smirked knowing she had just put Scarface in a situation that was sure to get physical in a matter of seconds. She had purposely told Scarface to arrive at her apartment around the time that she knew her super jealous boyfriend would be returning back from the supermarket. Scarface tried to play Mya for a fool and style on her as if he was the shit, but how quickly the tables had turned.

"Oh my God! Tyrone I'm so glad you are home," Mya said holding her chest for extra emphasis. She would have to pour it on thick if she wanted Tyrone to believe the story she was about to run down on him. "Remember my obsessed ex-boyfriend that I been telling you about?" She paused dramatically and caught her breath. "He just popped up at my door. I told him to leave, but he over powered me and forced his way inside demanding that I give him some pussy or he was going to take it. I'm so glad you came home when you did."

"Step to the side baby. I got this." Tyrone gently pushed Mya off to the side out of harm's way, and then ripped his wife beater off his body and tossed it to the floor as if he was Hulk Hogan. He flexed his muscles making one side of his chest jump and then the other while he stared Scarface down. The stare down continued, as Tyrone's hands became fist.

"So," Tyrone began. "I see you like taking advantage of defenseless women," he said taking a step forward.

"Yo listen; I ain't never had to take no pussy in my life. She called me over here trying to seduce me…"

"You a motherfucking lie!" Mya yelled from the sideline. She quickly cut Scarface off before the truth came out. "You're obsessed with me!"

"Bitch please! Ain't nobody obsessed with yo old raggedy ass," Scarface fumed looking at Mya as if she was crazy.

"Yo watch how the fuck you talk to my Shorty," Tyrone barked taking another step towards Scarface.

"You're Shorty?" Scarface gave Tyrone a sad look. "Listen man, I don't want no problems." He raised his hands in a surrendering motion. "You ain't got to ever worry about me talking to *Your Shorty*; ever again!" Scarface headed for the door, but Tyrone quickly blocked the exit.

Tyrone swung a quick haymaker; a punch intended to knock Scarface's head off. Scarface barely weaved the punch just in time to land a sharp three-punch combination to Tyrone's head and face. Tyrone let out a painful growl as his head rocked back and forth.

Scarface backed up and tried to use space to his benefit, but unfortunately, for him Mya had a small living room. He backed into the entertainment system and froze as a deer caught in headlights.

Tyrone landed two vicious body shots and then followed up with a mean uppercut that damn near lifted Scarface up off of his feet. Before Scarface got a chance to recover, Tyrone grabbed him by the throat and began strangling him. Scarface gasped and struggled to remove the big man's paws from around his neck. The two men went crashing through the small apartment like a tornado tearing up everything in its path.

Mya sat on the sideline with a smirk on her face. It was good to finally see Scarface get his ass whooped. Scarface put up a fight for as long as he could, but he was no match for his 6'8 opponent. Tyrone lifted Scarface above his head and then violently slammed him through the kitchen table that was made of glass.

"If you ever come around here stalking my Shorty again, I'mma murder ya stupid ass!" Tyrone punched Scarface in his face one last good time before grabbing him by his shirt and the waist of his jeans and tossing him out the front door like Jazzy Jeff from "The Fresh Prince of Bel-Air."

Scarface hit the ground hard and was instantly out like a light. Mya stood in the doorway of her apartment with an evil grin on her face. *"I bet you won't try to style on me no more,"* she thought as she slammed the door.

Chapter 20

"Ninety-eight, ninety-nine, one hundred," Angela counted out loud, removing her hand from the back of James' neck allowing him to come up for air. James head popped up out of the freezing cold lake water and his lungs sucked in as much air as they could as he gasped loudly. "You did well!"

"I could have went another twenty seconds," James lied breathing heavily. Angela's training course was kicking his ass, but he fought and did his best to complete it. He wanted to prove to her and himself that he could indeed hang with the big dogs and protect his woman if need be. So far, James had completed his hand-to-hand combat training as well as his high speed driving training. Now he was going through his holding his breath training and up next was knife training.

James sneezed loudly.

"You cold?"

James shook his head no. "Nah I'm good baby."

"Your body has to learn to adapt to the cold weather and the cold water temperature," Angela told him. "A simple sneeze can get you killed," she warned.

Angela gripped the back of James' head again. "You ready?"

James took a deep breath and then nodded his head. Angela quickly pushed his head down under the water. Angela felt bad for James. She knew she was being hard on him, but in order to teach him things that took her years to learn in a few months, she had to be hard on him. It was either that or take on The White Shadow alone, because there was no way she would let James go up against The White Shadow without the proper training.

Even though Angela was training James, she was still a little nervous about taking him out into the field with her. Training was one thing, but nothing compared to the real thing. Even though Angela was training James, she still planned on keeping a close eye on him.

She released the back of James' neck and again his head popped up out the water like a Jack-in-the-Box.

James head popped up out the water with a smile on his face. "This water is freezing. Why don't you come warm me up?" He said breathing heavily. He wrapped his hand around Angela's waist and then slid it down to her ass.

"Stay focused!" Angela roughly shoved James off of her. "I told you I'm not your girlfriend while we are training. You're going to have to keep your mind focused or else you gonna get yourself killed."

James nodded a silent apology as Angela shoved his head back down under the water. While he was under the water, James thought about the task that lied ahead and the seriousness of it. He knew that he would have to be at his best if he wanted to help Angela take down The White Shadow. James also knew that Angela was definitely going to need his help with this matter. He had seen The White Shadow in action, up close, and in person, and still he wasn't sure if he and Angela would be enough to stop the dangerous assassin.

The longer James stayed under the water, the more comfortable he was becoming being under water and holding his breath. James knew Angela would never back down from The White Shadow so he had to prepare himself as best he could to hold her down. From this point on, James promised to train as hard as he could and prepare his body as well as his mind for what was to come next.

Once the breathing training was complete, James made his way inside Angela's hideaway house and began his calisthenics followed by an hour of shadow boxing. James doubted that he and The White Shadow would ever do hand-to-hand combat, but he planned on being ready just in case. With Angela's teaching he was learning that it was better to be over prepared than under prepared.

Over on the sideline Angela stood watching James prepare himself for what was sure to be the fight and battle of his life. To say that she was proud of the progress that James was making would be an understatement. He was really trying and giving it his all. If they made it out of this situation alive, Angela planned on taking James on a much-needed, long vacation to spend some quality time with him and to cater to his needs.

James turned and spotted Angela standing leaning up against the wall with a 9mm in her gloved hand. He noticed Angela wore an all-black leather getup that hugged her curves nicely. "Am I doing that bad that you wanna put a bullet in my head?" He joked nodding down towards the gun that rested in Angela's hand. Angela stuck her 9mm down inside her holster, walked over, and kissed James on the lips. "I think you look so sexy when you sweat."

"Stay focused, please!" James gently pushed Angela back a few feet hitting her with a dose of her own medicine. "I'm not your man when I'm training, remember?" He teased.

"Forgive me," Angela purred while reaching down and grabbing James' manhood through his sweatpants. "Be ready for the fucking of a lifetime when I get back. You hear me?" She growled in James ear applying a little more pressure to his manhood.

"Is that a threat?" James countered smoothly looking down into Angela's eyes.

"That's a promise," Angela replied. She could feel James' manhood responding to her touch. "Be all cleaned up by the time I get back."

"Where you going?"

"To get us something to eat."

"Hurry up," James said and then kissed Angela's lips. "I miss you already."

"I shouldn't be longer than thirty minutes," Angela said pulling away from James. She knew if she stayed any longer that the two would wind up fucking each other's brains out and she would never make it to the store to get them some food. "Be ready when I get back."

"I love you!"

"I love you too," Angela, said exiting through the garage door. She grabbed a shiny black helmet with a dark tinted visor and slid it over her head. She revved the engine on her Yamaha

R-1 motorcycle and flew out of the garage like a bat out of hell onto the streets.

Angela watched as the speedometer reached 90 mph as she thought about how much she loved James. She could tell that James was finally letting his guards down and allowing her into his life. He was beginning to trust her more and more with each passing day.

Angela knew that it would be damn near impossible for her and James to live a normal life once this was said and done, but she planned on making life as simple and comfortable as possible for the both of them. If money could change and turn a fucked up situation into a better one then things might not be that bad because money was something that Angela had plenty of. She didn't know what the future had in store for her and James, but whatever it was, she planned on embracing it.

A shiny, black B.M.W. zooming past heading in the opposite direction snapped Angela out of her thoughts. She was riding at such a high speed that she wasn't able to get a look at the driver behind the wheel. Leaving James back at the house all alone had her a bit nervous. She knew James could protect himself if need be, but the fear of the unknown is what scared Angela the most.

"Let me hurry up and get this food so I can get back home to my man," Angela said to herself as she zoomed into the Wal-Mart parking lot.

Chapter 21

James stepped out the shower, dried himself off, and wrapped a towel around his waist as he looked at his reflection in the mirror and flexed his muscles for a few seconds. He was noticing that all the calisthenics were beginning to pay off handsomely. He knew that Angela was training him to become a killer, but deep down inside he knew that the only way the two of them would be able to work effectively together was if they both were on the same page. James knew there was no way that Angela would be able to cross over to his world, but he on the other hand was in the position to cross over into Angela's world. He also knew what he was signing up to do was wrong, but Angela was living proof that no matter what a person's occupation was, inside they still could be a beautiful person.

James' mind quickly went from stress to sex when he heard movement on the other side of the bathroom door. "Damn baby you got back quick." He stepped out the bathroom with a smile on his face. "You must really want some of this dick," James chuckled. Instantly, his laugh got caught in his throat and his heart dropped down to the pit of his stomach when he looked up and saw The White Shadow standing before him with a murderous look on his face. The fire that danced in The White Shadow's eyes told James exactly what he had planned for him.

"Angela," The White Shadow said in an angry tone. "Where is she?"

"Up my ass and around the corner," James replied. As soon as the words left his mouth, he knew he had just fucked up big time. The White Shadow nodded his head and slowly began moving towards James. James took a fighting stance. The only thing that covered his nakedness was a towel. Now he understood why Angela carried a gun with her everywhere she went, even in the bathroom. It was situations like this where it was better to be over prepared rather than under prepared.

Once in striking distance, James fired a quick jab that The White Shadow easily slipped and landed a devastating punch to James' ribs. The blow buckled James, but he managed to somehow keep his footing.

James fired a sharp hook aimed for The White Shadow's chin with the swiftness of a cat. The White Shadow ducked the punch by dropping down into a full split and countered with a quick uppercut that landed under James' towel in between his legs.

The blow forced James' face to crumble up in pain as he dropped down to his knees with his hands clutching his manhood. The White Shadow slowly hopped back up to his feet, grabbed the back of James' head, and fired off two vicious knee strikes that rearranged James once handsome face. James rolled around on the floor in severe pain. Now the towel that was once wrapped around his waist had been removed exposing his nakedness.

James made a weak attempt to crawl back up to his feet, but a boot to his face put him back on his backside.

"Get up and fight me like a man," The White Shadow taunted. "I know the so called "Teflon Queen" taught you more than this," he said circling James like a shark that smelled blood. The White Shadow didn't know why Mr. Biggz had put a contract on the Agent and honestly, he didn't care. In his eyes,

James was nothing more than an easy payday. "Are you going to tell me where Angela is or are you going to make me kill you?"

James didn't reply. He struggled back up to his feet, but before he could even make a move, a round house kick to his face put him right back on his backside again.

"Since you don't want to talk, how about you deliver a message for me?" The White Shadow removed an ink pen from his pocket along with a small piece of paper and scribbled down a message for The Teflon Queen. "You make sure you tell that bitch I'm tired of playing with her and that I'll be expecting to hear from her real soon," The White Shadow huffed as he removed a throwing knife from the small of his back. In a quick motion, he placed the note on James' chest and then jammed the knife through the piece of paper. He watched as James' eyes widened with shock and fear. James felt the sharp pain in his chest, but it still hadn't registered in his brain yet. It took a second for his brain to finally process what was going on, but by the time it finally registered it was too late.

The White Shadow threw a quick open palmed blow that broke James nose and sent the broken bone up into his brain killing him instantly. James lifeless naked body laid on the floor with blood running out of his chest and nose. Once the mission at hand was complete, The White Shadow turned and exited the house just as quiet as he had entered leaving a dead body with a note attached behind to be recovered.

* * * *

Angela pulled back up into the garage and killed the engine on her bike. She had only been away from James for a couple of minutes and she was already missing him like crazy. Every second away from James felt like an hour. On the ride back to the house, Angela was beginning to wonder how she had made it without James all those years before meeting him. How she did it was a mystery to her because now she couldn't even see her life without James in it. Life without James wasn't life at all to Angela. She didn't do a lot of praying, but since getting James back in her life Angela had begun praying more often. She was praying more for James than herself, but at the end of the day, she depended and relied on herself to look after James and keep him safe.

"I got your favorite; a twenty piece nuggets and fries. They didn't have no more sweet and sour sauce so I got you barbecue instead," Angela sang happily as she turned the corner and saw James sprawled out across the floor butt naked with a knife sticking out of his chest.

"Oh my God... No! No! No!" She ran over to James body, dropped down to her knees, and checked to see if he had a pulse. Once Angela was sure that James was dead, she looked up to the ceiling and released a loud pain filled scream as big crocodile tears rolled down her cheeks. Immediately, she regretted leaving James in the house all alone and getting him caught up in her bullshit. She blamed herself for his death. In between sobs, Angela looked down and noticed that the knife inserted in James' chest held a small note in place.

Angela removed the knife from James' chest and began reading it.

"If you're looking for me, I'll be at the address below... Don't disappoint... P.S. Your boyfriend cried and begged for his life like a little bitch before he died."

Angela's eyes immediately teared up after reading the note. Sadness didn't cause the tears, anger did. Murderous thoughts filled Angela's mind. She was definitely going to make The White Shadow pay for what he had done to James. Angela looked down and noticed that James' eyes were still open staring out into space. She bent over, kissed James on his forehead, and gently shut his eyes. "I love you James and I promise I won't let The White Shadow get away with this," she whispered.

Angela stood up and headed straight for her gun closet. She held the small note as all the different makes and models of guns stared back at her. The White Shadow wanted The Teflon Queen and that's just what he was about to get.

Chapter 22

Vicky stood in the bathroom giving herself a once over in the bathroom mirror. Tonight was the night when Bone would take his last breath. Vicky had called Bone, told him that she was hungry, and wanted to go out to get something to eat and some drinks. Little did Bone know that Vicky had already made a call to the goons that Scarface assigned to take care of the situation as soon as their call ended.

Two cars filled with shooters sat parked across the street waiting on Bone's arrival. On the inside, Vicky felt kind of bad for setting Bone up. Within the past week, the two had been hooking up rather frequently not to mention the sex was amazing and the best Vicky had ever had. Her feelings were beginning to grow for Bone more and more with each passing day, but this wasn't about feelings. This was about business. Bone had violated Scarface and Shekia, and for that, he had to be dealt with accordingly.

Vicky had been paid in advance to do a job and it was too late to turn back now. No matter how much she was beginning to fall for Bone, she knew what she had to do. Vicky flinched and let out a low suppressed squeal when the sound of multiple gunshots could be heard ringing out. Her hotel room was located on the seventh floor and she could still hear the thunderous sound of the gunshots. The gunfire paused momentarily, and then picked back up a few seconds later.

The gunshots notified Vicky of Bone's arrival. She did her best to ignore the gunshots as she began packing away her belongings. Her purpose for being in New York had been served and now Vicky could get back to the nice sunny weather and palm trees in Miami.

* * * *

Bone sate behind the wheel of his black Benz with dark tinted windows with a frown on his face. In his hand sat several pictures of Vicky. These were not regular pictures, but pictures of her all hugged up on another man, pictures of her and this other man from past to present, and pictures that spoke a thousand words. Bone recognized the man in the pictures as the man Capo had introduced him to a while ago, the same man that the streets called Scarface.

After taking the time to put two and two together, Bone discovered that Vicky wasn't who she said she was.

"I told you I didn't trust that bitch," Mike Murder said from the passenger seat. He never liked or trusted Vicky and to him she was the worst type of woman in the world. She was a lying ass bitch!

"Where you said you found these pictures at again?" Bone handed the pictures back to Mike Murder. On the inside, he felt like a fool. He slowly but surely was beginning to open up to Vicky and now she had fucked all that up by lying.

"Those shits was on her Instagram page." Mike Murder shook his head sadly. He could care less about Vicky. As far as he was concerned, she was a good as dead. "So what now?"

"I got something for this sneaky ass bitch," Bone said as two of his goons pulled up beside the Benz in an old school beat up Station Wagon. Immediately, the four men swapped rides.

Bone and Mike Murder hopped in the Station Wagon while the two goons hopped in the Benz.

"Yo, I'm supposed to meet this chick at that fancy hotel a few blocks away. I need you two to ride over there and let me know if some fishy shit is going on or not," Bone yelled across to the driver. "Y'all niggas strapped right?"

The tugged out looking goon behind the wheel of the Benz nodded his head. "You already know!" With that being said, Bone watched as the Benz pulled out into traffic heading towards the hotel.

Bone hadn't even fully pulled all the way into his parking spot across the street from the hotel when two cars filled with shooters pulled up and opened fire on the Benz.

Bone and Mike Murder watched as bullets rocked and rattled the Benz, turning the luxury car into Swiss cheese. Then suddenly the sound of tires squealing and burning robber filled the air and like that, the two cars filled with shooters were gone.

Bone looked over at Mike Murder. "I'm about to violate this bitch!"

* * * *

Vicky packed up her things as fast as she could. She had wanted to leave the hotel room before the police and ambulances arrived on the scene, and especially before any of Bone's flunkies caught wind of his assassination and began to put two and two together. She planned on leaving the hotel like a thief in the night and never stepping foot back in the state of New York ever again. That was until a sharp stern knock at the door caused her to look over at the door as if it was an U.F.O. The second knock was even louder and stronger than the first one.

"Who…who is it?" Vicky called out in a timid voice. Seconds later, the hotel room door came crashing open and in stepped Bone flanked by Mike Murder.

"Bitch stop playing stupid! You know who the fuck it is!" Bone barked storming inside the room with his .40 cal in his hand. Caught off guard, Vicky knew she had to think fast and decided to put her acting skills to the test.

"Oh my God," she gasped grabbing her chest. "I heard the shots… I'm just so glad that you are alright," she faked rushing into Bone's arms. Vicky had her performance down packed and she even managed to shed a few tears in the process. If this were a casting call or an audition, she would have definitely gotten the part hands down. "I was so worried about you," she cried.

"Is that right?" Bone asked gently moving Vicky back to a comfortable distance. "So why you ain't call me to make sure I was alright?"

"I… I… I was just about to call, but the shots were so loud they kind of startled me," Vicky said going off the top of her head and making it up as she went along.

"What happened to us going to dinner?"

"I was waiting on you. You see I was already dressed," Vicky said. She tried her hardest not to stumble over her words. She knew with one slip of the tongue that her ass was grass.

Bone looked over at Vicky's luggage all neatly packed and sitting by the door. "I see you got your bags all packed." He paused for extra emphasis. "Planned on going somewhere?"

"Not without you I wasn't."

"This bitch is full of shit!" Mike Murder butted in form the sideline. He was sick and tired of Vicky's lies and he couldn't stand the sound of her voice any longer.

Vicky spun around as if she was ready to fight. "Last time I checked, nobody was talking to you so do me a favor and mind your fucking business!"

The next thing Vicky knew, she was being awaken by a warm liquid splashing on her face followed by laughter. She opened her eyes, looked up, and saw Bone standing over her wide legged holding his penis in his hand.

"Why…why are you doing this?" Vicky mumbled raising her hand attempting to block the urine from splashing directly onto her face.

Bone raised his foot and brought the heel of his boot down across Vicky's nose breaking it. He did that to shut her up. "You must not have heard about me." He chuckled as he watched Vicky squirm around on the floor in pure agony. "I'm the last person you want to fuck with in case you ain't know so!"

"Wait!" Vicky pleaded with her hand covering her broken nose with blood spilling down in between her fingers. "I got money… Whatever you want; it's yours…"

Bone and Mike Murder broke out into a strong laugh.

"This bitch is bugged out!" Mike Murder called out.

Bone reached out and roughly grabbed Vicky by her hair causing her head to jerk back in the process.

"Please don't do this to me," Vicky pleaded. Her eyes begged Bone to leave her alone and allow her to keep her life.

"I didn't," Bone smirked. "You did it to yourself!" He tightly held Vicky's hair, grabbed the back of her jeans, and spun her around tossing her into the floor to ceiling window. Vicky's body hit the window with such force that the window cracked and her momentum sent her flying through the seventh floor window down on to the unforgiving concrete.

"Stupid ass bitch," Bone said looking down at Vicky's dead body sprawled out down below by the front entrance of the hotel.

"What now?" Mike Murder asked eager to keep the party going.

"Now we send a few shooters out to Miami to pay that clown Scarface a visit."

Chapter 23

"What happened to your face?" Shekia asked Scarface as soon as he stepped foot inside their bedroom. Before he had left home he was in one piece, and now he looked as if he had been jumped by an entire gang.

"Mya set me up and her man attacked me," Scarface said not bothering to go into details.

"Huh?" Shekia said with a confused look on her face. "Mya set you up? You went over to her house?"

"It's a long story," Scarface said as he picked up his cell phone and called up one of his main goons and demanded that he be there within the next fifteen minutes. Scarface ended the call, looked up, and saw Shekia staring at him. "What?"

"What?" Shekia repeated with her arms folded across her chest. "Well you can start by telling me what you were doing over at Mya's house for starters."

"I ain't got time for this shit," Scarface said waving Shekia off. He wasn't in the mood to hear her mouth at the moment. He had way too much shit going on right now to feed into what she was getting ready to complain about.

"You ain't got time for what I'm talking about or you ain't got time for me?" Shekia wanted him to be specific. She felt like she had the right to ask Scarface whatever she wanted since he was her man.

"Both!" Was Scarface's response.

"Really?" Shekia yelled. "That's how you feel!"

"Listen bitch, I don't want to hear all that crying shit right now," Scarface barked. "You see I got a lot going on right now and you wanna question a nigga. Fuck Outta Here!"

Shekia couldn't believe that Scarface had fixed his lips to speak to her like that, like she was a piece of trash, and like he didn't give a fuck if she came or went. What hurt the most was Shekia would have never spoke to him in that manner no matter how mad he made her. Shekia stood there waiting to see if Scarface would realize that he had made a mistake and apologize, but instead he continued his rant.

"Why the fuck you standing there looking stupid for?" Scarface continued.

"Why are you talking to me like this? Do you not love me no more?" Shekia asked with her face wet from all the tears that were streaming down her face.

The sound of the doorbell ringing caused Scarface to walk out the room leaving Shekia standing in the bedroom alone.

Downstairs Scarface saw ten goons standing around in the den loud talking and laughing as if they didn't have a care in the world. Immediately, he explained to his team what had happened and how he wanted the situation to be handled. While Scarface was explaining everything to his team, he noticed Shekia coming down the stairs. Oversized designer shades covered her eyes and in each had she held a duffle bag. The sound of her flip-flops slapping against the floor seemed to grab Scarface's attention. He watched as she walked by as if she didn't even know him and she walked right out the front door.

"Give me a second," Scarface said to his team as he ran outside to catch Shekia before she left. "Yo, hold up!" He jogged across the yard finally catching up with Shekia.

"No," Shekia huffed. She tried to open the driver door to her Audi, but Scarface stood in front of the door denying her access.

"So, as soon as shit gets hard, you just gone run out on us?" Scarface pressed.

"I can't," Shekia said, attempting to enter her vehicle, but again Scarface denied her access.

"You can't what?"

"I can't do this no more," Shekia yelled in Scarface's face. "This relationship isn't fifty/fifty. You running around here keeping secrets and talking to me as if I'm garbage. You're not the same man I met months ago. You've changed and not for the better."

"Yo, listen…"

"No, I'm tired of listening!" Shekia barked. She was tired of Scarface and his bullshit. She felt as though her feelings didn't matter to him anymore. He didn't even love her enough to take the time out to listen to her. "I don't want to be with you no more! I hate you!"

That last statement caught Scarface off guard and stung. No matter how mad Shekia had made him, he never hated her or wished any bad on her so to hear those words came as a shock to him. "You don't mean that Shekia… Why don't you go back in the house and we'll talk about this later," he tried to reason.

"Why were you over at Mya's house, huh?" Shekia pressed letting her jealousy get the best of her. The thought of Scarface with another woman drove Shekia crazy and right now he had her blood boiling on the inside and ready to kill something.

"So that's what this is all about?" Scarface frowned. "I come home with my face bashed in and all you care about is what I was doing over at Mya's house?" He couldn't believe what he was hearing.

"You damn right," Shekia said with much attitude. In her eyes, there was no reason for her man to be at another woman's house. "You still can't answer the question. What were you doing over at your ex's house, huh? And here I was like a fool thinking that you were different. You ain't no different from the rest of these no good niggas out here," she disrespected. "Can I leave now?"

Scarface gave Shekia a sad look, moved out from in front of the driver door of the Audi, and headed back inside. He couldn't believe some of the things that came out of Shekia's mouth, but at least he knew how she really felt about him. At the moment, Scarface didn't have time to focus on Shekia and her foolishness. Right now, he had bigger fish to fry. He went back in the house, rounded up his goons, and headed out.

* * * *

Mya sat curled up in Tyrone's lap on the couch as the two enjoyed the new block Bbuster that starred Denzel Washington. "I love that nigga Denzel," Mya stated plainly. It was something about watching Scarface get his ass whipped that seemed to put her at ease. Mya didn't feel bad for setting Scarface up. If he wanted to be with that raggedy looking chick she had seen over at his house, then he deserved to get his ass whipped. The ass whipping that her new boo Tyrone gave Scarface replayed over and over in Mya's mind and the vision caused a smile to form on her face.

A loud boom followed by the front door being kicked open caused Tyrone and Mya both to jump in fear. At that very moment, they knew they had fucked up and violated the wrong motherfucker.

Several wild looking goons stormed inside the small apartment. A goon that weighed close to three hundred pounds walked directly over to Mya and punched her in her face. The punch sounded like a .22 had been fired inside the apartment. Then he roughly grabbed Mya and violently slammed her down to the floor placing a steel-toed boot on the back of her neck. The rest of the goons roughly manhandled Tyrone. They tossed him around as if he was a woman and put hands and feet on him until finally Scarface walked in.

"What's this all about gentleman?" Tyrone asked through a pair of bloody lips.

"You know what the fuck this is about," Scarface said removing a .357 from his waistband.

Tyrone wiped the blood from his mouth with the back of his hand and then flashed a bloody smile. "Oh word?" He stared directly at Scarface. "I thought you was an official nigga," he laughed. "You ain't nothing but one of these young punks out here who can't take an ass whipping... You talk all that tough shit and then when a nigga punch you in your mouth, the first thing you wanna do is go pick up a gun. You aren't no man! You a punk and I'm glad I put my foot in yo ass! That's what you get for trying to rape my Shorty!"

The word rape sent Scarface over the edge. "Nigga didn't I tell you I ain't rape nobody!" He barked as he ran over and backslapped Tyrone across the face with his .357. "You wanna be one of these save a hoe niggas, right?" Scarface blacked out and pistol-whipped Tyrone until his face was nothing but a bloody pulp.

Over on the sideline Mya cried her eyes out as she was forced to watch Scarface brutally beat Tyrone's once handsome face in with the butt of his gun. She wasn't crying because Scarface had damn near killed Tyrone, she was crying because she knew that she was next and by the look on Scarface's face, she didn't know how far he would go.

"Boss man what you want us to do with her?" The three hundred pound goon that stood with his foot on Mya's neck asked. The big man made sure he put most of his weight and intense pressure on Mya's neck.

"Put that bitch in the trunk. I got something special in mind for her," Scarface ordered. He fired two rounds down into Tyrone's chest, turned, and exited the apartment.

Scarface slid in the back seat of the Cadillac truck that waited curbside for him. As soon as the back door slammed shut, the Cadillac truck pulled away from the curb.

In the backseat, Scarface helped himself to a glass of vodka with no chaser. After the type of day he had, he needed a drink. He took a slow sip of the liquid fire and made an ugly face as he checked his phone to see if Shekia had called or texted him. Shekia pissed him off and disrespected Scarface, but despite all that, he still loved her dearly. After thinking over the situation Scarface realized that what the two of them were fighting over was foolish and nonsense. He asked himself if losing a good woman worth was what he was mad or upset about. Every time he asked himself the question, the answer always remained the same. He didn't want to lose Shekia and he knew if he didn't do anything to stop her, she would be gone forever.

"Fuck that! I ain't losing my baby over this bullshit," Scarface said to himself as he grabbed his phone. Just as he got ready to dial Shekia's number, his cell phone vibrated in his hand. Scarface glanced down at the caller I.D. and noticed that he didn't recognize the number, but still he answered. "Yo, who dis?"

"What up, this Black," the caller said identifying himself. Black was one of Scarface's most ruthless goons and reliable shooters.

"My nigga Black, what up? I hope you calling me to tell me that, that Bone situation has been taken care of," Scarface said taking another sip from his cup. Silence fell upon them for a few seconds. "Black, you still there?"

"Yeah I'm here," Black said in a low tone.

"What's up? Did you take care of that Bone situation for me?" Scarface asked again.

"We Swiss cheesed his whip, but that clown wasn't inside," Black told him. "But that's not what I called you for. I called to talk to you about Vicky."

"What's up with her? I haven't had a chance to call her. I had a few things that needed my immediate attention," Scarface said. "But what's up with Vicky?" Again, silence fell upon the two men.

"Vicky is dead," Black said putting it out there not wanting to prolong or sugarcoat the situation any further than he already had.

"What you mean she's dead?" Scarface said hoping he heard wrong, but with his current streak of luck he knew he had heard right.

"Bone caught on to what she was up to," Black said sadly. "He whipped her ass, and then threw her out of her seven story hotel room window."

"You're kidding me, right? Please tell me that you are joking!" Scarface's tone rose as his eyes filled with tears. At the moment, he felt like he had the worst luck in the world.

"I'm sorry," was all that Black could say. Scarface ended the call and cried his heart out. He knew it was because of him that his little sister was dead. If he hadn't involved Vicky in the bullshit beef that him and Bone had, she would still be alive right now.

"Shekia told me to just leave it alone to begin with," Scarface, scolded himself. He blamed himself and beat himself up as if everything that had happened was his fault. Before Scarface could even digest the news of his sister being murdered, his cell phone vibrated in his hand once again. Again, he didn't recognize the number that flashed across his screen, but Scarface answered it anyway hoping that maybe it was Shekia calling to ask him to come pick her up from the airport.

"Yo, who dis?" He answered doing his best to hide the pain in his voice.

"Yes, I'm looking for a Mr. Johnson," a soft woman's voice said on the other line.

"Yeah, this is he," Scarface answered skeptically. Not a lot of people knew his last name so his antennas were on full alert right now.

"Hi, my name is Ms. Foye and I'm a nurse at Mount Sinai Medical Center and a Shekia Richardson was just in a bad car accident. She asked that I call and notify you before she lost consciousness."

"Is she alright?" Scarface asked with his voice filled with panic and concern.

"I'm not sure of her condition right now sir. Our staff is doing all they can as we speak," Nurse Foye told him.

"I'm on my way!" Scarface hung up in the nurse's ear. He yelled to his driver to take him to the Mount Sinai Medical Center.

Scarface was living out a real life nightmare. It seemed like everyone close to him was dying or damn near dying and it was all his fault and on top of that, it was nothing he could do to stop it.

"Boss man," the driver said looking at Scarface through the rearview mirror. "We got company."

Scarface turned and looked out the rear window and immediately flashing blue and red lights assaulted his eyes. "Fuck!" He cursed loudly.

"What you want me to do, Boss man?" The driver asked. His eyes said that he hoped that Scarface told him to take the pigs on a high-speed chase, but today wouldn't be his lucky day.

"Pull this bitch over," Scarface ordered and then extended his .357 pass the driver's shoulder handing him the firearm. The driver quickly slid the gun in the glove compartment.

A red-faced racist police officer walked over to the driver side window of the Cadillac and banged on it loudly with his nightstick.

The driver rolled down his window and immediately his eyes were assaulted by the bright light of the officer's flashlight. "Is there a problem, officer?"

"I ask the questions around here.... Boy!" The officer shot back.

"We have any emergency, officer. We were heading to the hospital because my girlfriend just got into a bad car accident. We're sorry if we did anything wrong. We're really in a rush... Like I said, it's an emergency," Scarface said in a polite, but urgent and firm tone of voice.

"You said your girlfriend was just in a car accident?" The officer asked looking over at Scarface.

"Yes sir."

"Step out of the car, please?"

"Huh?"

"Sir, I said step out of the car!" The officer yelled with his hand moving to his holstered service pistol.

Scarface sighed loudly as him and his driver both stepped out of the vehicle and placed their hands on the hood of the S.U.V. Before the officer got a chance to say another word, his Walkie Talkie went off informing him of a shooting that had just taken place not too far from their exact location.

Once Scarface heard the officer's Walkie Talkie go off, he knew that he was fucked. Seconds later, three more cop cars pulled up to the scene.

After putting two and two together, Scarface and his driver were immediately hand cuffed and placed in the back seat of one of the squad cars.

Scarface sadly looked out the window as the officers searched his truck. Once they began searching the truck, Scarface knew it was just a matter of time before they found his gun. It only took the officers three minutes to find the .357 in the glove compartment. As Scarface was taken off to jail, the only thing that was on his mind was Shekia.

Chapter 24

The White Shadow stood alone in the abandoned warehouse. Strapped to his shoulder was a Sub Ruger-MP9 machine gun. The abandoned warehouse was the address that he left on the note for Angela and if he knew Angela as well as he thought he did, he knew it would only be a matter of time before she showed up ready for war.

The White Shadow looked forward to the showdown between him and the legendary Teflon Queen. He was getting tired of Angela. She always seemed to slip through the cracks and escape by the skin on her teeth. It was as if the bitch had nine lives and was an expert at surviving. But as soon as Angela showed up that was all going to change. The White Shadow would make sure of that.

He envisioned in his mind several different ways of how he would end Angela's life. Each vision was more brutal than the previous one. He knew that once he killed her Agent boyfriend that Angela would be gunning for him and that's exactly what he wanted. In the back of The White Shadow's mind he hoped that when Angela did arrive, she would be emotional from the loss of her boyfriend and move sloppy and recklessly. That way he could use her emotions to his advantage.

Out in the distance, The White Shadow could hear something that sounded like a speedboat, but due to the fact that they weren't in the middle of the sea, he knew the noise he heard wasn't coming from a speedboat. With each second that passed, the noise grew louder and louder until finally The White Shadow spotted something out in the distance heading directly towards him at a super natural speed.

The White Shadow didn't know what it was, but he knew that it was The Teflon Queen. She had showed up just as he had expected her to. The White Shadow had done a great job luring Angela into the warehouse. Little did she know if everything went according to The White Shadow's plan, she wouldn't be leaving the warehouse alive.

* * * *

The speedometer on Angela's motorcycle read 110 mph. The engine roared loudly as the machine in between her legs heated up. Angela knew that once her and The White Shadow locked horns, that only one of them would be left standing. It would be a test of skills and it would all come down to who wanted to continue breathing more.

Angela knew what was at stake and she was more than ready to get revenge for her man. She knew it wasn't going to be easy, but she planned on going out with a bang. The White Shadow was the *"so called"* best assassin in the world, but today his skills were definitely going to be put to the test; the ultimate test and Angela was bringing her A-game.

The louder the engine roared, the closer the warehouse became. The anticipation alone was enough to drive Angela crazy. Goosebumps covered her body and perspiration covered her face.

Angela didn't know what lay ahead in the warehouse and frankly, she didn't care. Her main concern was getting to The White Shadow. James' death was weighing heavy on her heart and to this minute Angela still wished that she could go back in time and somehow save James or even protect him better. A good man was dead because of her and that was something that Angela was going to have to live with for the rest of her life.

The closer Angela got, she noticed that there was an opening in the warehouse big enough for a tractor-trailer to fit in. Angela guided her bike and headed straight for the opening. The speedometer was now reading 120 mph.

Angela zoomed through the opening and immediately the sound of automatic gunfire could be heard. Angela quickly grabbed the Tech-9 attached to the back of her bike, hit the back brakes, and came to a long, noisy, dramatic, skidding stop. As soon as she spotted The White Shadow, she opened fire on him.

With the swiftness of a cat, The White Shadow took cover behind some old looking barrels that decorated the warehouse.

Angela quickly dropped her bike and ducked behind a wall. Behind the wall, she removed her motorcycle helmet so she could see better.

"So glad you could finally make it!" She heard The White Shadow yell. The walls in the warehouse were causing his voice to echo.

Angela didn't reply. She crouched down with a firm two-handed grip on her Tech-9 and moved around the warehouse quieter than a mouse. Angela crept around to the other side of the warehouse making sure she stayed as low as possible. She crept alongside the barrels trying to get the drop on her opponent. Angela heard a crunch of gravel, which gave her an idea where The White Shadow was so she popped up, and fired at the sound.

Over on the other side of the warehouse bullets struck several barrels. The shots drove The White Shadow out form his hiding place. Angela tried to gun The White Shadow down while he was exposed, but just as quickly as he appeared, he disappeared.

In a split second, twelve rapid shots hit and ricocheted off the barrel that Angela was behind rattling her. The shots came too close to home for her liking. She quickly sprung from her hiding spot recklessly firing shots over her shoulder as a trail of bullets followed her. Angela ran and dove through a wooden door that led to a small room that once upon a time was used as an office.

"Shit!" Angela cursed as multiple gunshots blew through the wooden office as if it was made out of paper. She kept her back to the wall and reloaded her weapon in four seconds flat.

Then suddenly all the gunfire came to a stop and Angela could hear The White Shadow's voice.

"Angela!" The White Shadow yelled. "Let's settle this like professionals." Angela heard him yell. She wasn't sure if he was trying to trick her or not, so she didn't move from her hiding spot. She didn't trust The White Shadow one bit.

"Gladiator style! What do you say?" The White Shadow yelled coming from out of his hiding spot. "Let's see who's really number one?"

"Fuck you," Angela yelled back. She didn't trust The White Shadow and she knew there was no way both of them would leave this warehouse alive.

The White Shadow tossed his machine gun down to the floor. "Me and you one on one, hand to hand, and knife to knife."

Angela swiftly sprung from out of the office with her weapon trained on The White Shadow. "Don't move!"

The White Shadow ignored Angela, removed his backup 9mm, and tossed it to the floor. He then removed his bulletproof suit jacket, followed by his bulletproof shirt, and tossed them both down to the floor. He stood before Angela shirtless with leather gloves on. The look on his face told Angela he was ready for war.

Thunder boomed through the sky as a heavy downpour of rain began outside. The rain was beating on the roof of the warehouse a hundred drops per second.

Angela stood with her Tech-9 aimed at The White Shadow's head. His well-built body and chiseled six-pack was a sight to see. The thought of blowing The White Shadow's head off crossed her mind a few times. Angela had to fight herself to not paint the floor with his brains. As bad as she wanted to shoot The White Shadow, that's not how she wanted to defeat him; especially while he was unarmed. When she killed him, she wanted it to be a clean kill. Reluctantly Angela tossed her Tech-9 down to the floor. Then she slowly removed her two silenced .380s.

The White Shadow watched Angela's every move closely. Angela slowly removed her shirt, followed by her custom-made Teflon vest. She slowly tossed them both down to the floor. She stood before The White Shadow wearing a black sports bra, black army pants, black boots, black leather gloves, and on her wrist rested a black bracelet.

"Let's take this outside, shall we?" The White Shadow suggested. Angela knew the only reason The White Shadow wanted to take the battle outside was to make sure neither one of them had any access to the weapons they had just tossed to the floor.

Angela silently agreed as the two made their way out into the pouring rain. Outside rain fell like rocks and it was cold rain to add on to the already cold weather. Angela stepped out into the rain and she could instantly see her breath through the cold.

The White Shadow and Angela faced off preparing to do battle, and then out of nowhere The White Shadow reached behind his back and removed a knife with a blade sharp enough to cut through bones. An evil smirk appeared on The White Shadow's face as he came at Angela hard and fast with fury and anger. He tried to stab Angela at short range. Angela quickly backed away and twisted using her footwork to get out of the way. She barely made it out of stabbing range. The White Shadow was persistent and good with a knife. The rain was making it difficult for Angela to keep a close eye on the sharp blade in The White Shadow's hand.

Angela tried to slap his wrist and force him to drop the knife as she back peddled through mud and puddles of dirty water. The White Shadow danced, bobbed and weaved, and feinted as if he was about to charge Angela in order to throw her off and keep her off balance. He wanted to keep her on the defensive until the business end of his knife found a home in her flesh.

There wasn't much Angela could do. She didn't have nowhere to run. The best she could do was control how she got cut or where she would be stabbed.

The White Shadow faked low with the knife and came up high with a sharp hook to Angela's jaw. The punch shook Angela up, but she managed to somehow keep her footing. She could take a punch. It was the blade that concerned her the most.

The Whites Shadow feinted again, but this time Angela fell for the swift movement and The White Shadow went in for the kill. He swung the knife with extreme force at Angela's throat. At that moment, everything seemed to move in slow motion, so slowly that Angela could see every separate raindrop.

She could have counted each one before it touched the ground. She weaved leaning back as far as she could trying to get as far away from the blade as possible. The blade missed Angela's throat by a fingernail, but make contact with her chest leaving a nasty cut behind that began to bleed almost instantly.

The White Shadow's movements made it hard for Angela to figure out his style. His feints were swift and unbalancing. His movements made Angela believe that he was born with a knife in his hand at birth.

The White Shadow moved with arrogance and patience while Angela moved as if death was near. While The White Shadow cockily danced around, Angela tapped the button on her bracelet and a four-inch blade appeared in the palm of her gloved hand like magic.

The White Shadow moved swiftly and tried to stab Angela in the heart, but she quickly sidestepped the knife strike and brought up the four-inch blade, a blade he had not seen. Angela caught him off guard. She made contact with his right forearm and opened up his skin. She tried to cut him down to the bone. The White Shadow quickly backed away. He was shocked by Angela's speed and shocked to see that she had a weapon. The pain from his cut stunned him. The cut was so bad that The White Shadow had to switch the knife over to his left hand; his not so good hand.

Now he danced a brand new dance, one with less arrogance and swagger. His deep frown told Angela that he wasn't used to being the one on the business end of a sharp blade.

Again, The White Shadow stabbed at Angela. He threw a series of jabs with his knife leading the way. Angela caught The

White Shadow's knife hand and bent it at the wrist forcing him to drop his knife down into the mud. She then landed a bone-breaking elbow to The White Shadow's nose. This blow stunned him and sent him stumbling a few steps backwards. The rain and mud were compromising his footing. The White Shadow quickly went from the one doing the attacking to the one being attacked. His offense had desperately turned into defense.

The tables had turned and now Angela was the one holding the blade and The White Shadow stood weaponless.

"Come on bitch! Let's do this!" The White Shadow growled. There was no backing down in him and definitely not one weak bone in his body. If he was in it, he was in it to the death. That's just the way he was trained from birth. Angela charged at The White Shadow with her blade in her hand. She was tired of playing and ready to finish this battle once and for all. She tried to plunge the end of her blade in The White Shadow's chest, but he quickly jumped back and caught Angela's wrist in mid swing. They fought for the knife in her hand, a knife sharp enough to kill.

While Angela and The White Shadow struggled, her combat boots were slipping and his field boots were sliding. The two battled across the wet concrete wrestling eye-to-eye.

Angela gritted her teeth, grunted, and shoved the blade towards The White Shadow's chest. She struggled with him, strength against strength. They were in the midst of an arm wrestle that neither assassin wanted to lose. They both knew that losing meant death.

The White Shadow landed a vicious knee to the pit of Angela's stomach. The blow caused her to double over in pain and her grip on her knife loosened. The White Shadow took advantage of the situation and threw a quick rabbit punch that landed in the center of Angela's throat forcing her to drop the knife. She tried to hurry up and pick the knife back up, but The White Shadow quickly kicked it out of her reach.

Angela backed up and took a fighting stance. Then in a blind rage, The White Shadow went after Angela. She didn't back down, but instead she moved toward the fight not away from it. She started throwing spearing elbows and knees at a relentless pace. She gave just as good as she got. She took one punch to land two.

The White Shadow fired a quick jab that snapped Angela's head back and followed up with a hook that Angela saw coming, but didn't have enough energy to block or avoid. He hit her the way a man should never hit a woman. The hook connected on Angela's chin and sent her crashing down to the wet concrete. The White Shadow quickly hopped on top of Angela and began throwing punches from all angles like a U.F.C. cage fighter.

Angela tried to bob and weave. She did her best to block the onslaught of vicious blows. Several hard blows broke through Angela's guard causing one of her eyes to close up completely shut.

Angela bucked her midsection up and somehow got The White Shadow up off of her. She staggered back up to her feet half-dazed and was only able to see out of one eye. Just like The White Shadow, there was no quit in Angela. If you wanted her to stop, then you had to kill her; plain and simple.

Angela ran and went airborne taking her knee straight to The White Shadow's wounded face. Angela hit him hard and then went down hard too. She crashed hard landing on the unforgiving rocks and concrete.

Angela quickly crawled back up to her feet and moved towards The White Shadow. She landed an eight-punch combination to his stomach, ribs, and back. She went to work on his body in hopes of slowing him down. The White Shadow got in close, grabbed Angela's head, tried to send a knee deep into her stomach, but she twisted before his knee could find its target. Angela and The White Shadow wrestled and grappled. They tussled until they both went down to the wet ground making a big loud splash sending water flying everywhere. While on the ground, Angela and The White Shadow both struggled and fought for positioning. The White Shadow slipped in a few stiff punches in the process. Dirt, grit, and mud covered both Angela and The White Shadow's bodies as they rolled around on the ground. During the struggle, Angela managed to get a good grip on The White Shadow's arm. She swiftly lifted her legs and wrapped them around The White Shadow's neck putting him in a scissors maneuver. She then took The White Shadow's arm and placed it in an arm bar. This is a submission move that if done right could break a man's arm or rip it straight from the socket.

"Arrgggg!" The Whites Shadow shrieked as Angela applied pressure to the arm bar. From the way The White Shadow screamed, Angela could tell that The White Shadow was in excruciating pain. This was probably the most pain he had ever been in during his entire life.

Angela applied extreme pressure on The White Shadow's arm until she finally heard it snap!

Angela slowly stood to her feet and watched as The White Shadow rolled around in the mud in agony. Severe pain resided in his blue eyes. Like a wounded animal, The White Shadow slowly crawled back up to his feet with his right arm dangling loosely by his side. The angered look on his bloodied and swollen face told Angela that he wasn't going to stop coming at her. Blood was dripping from his nose down on his puffy lips and he had a murderous look in his eyes.

"It's over," Angela said feeling sorry for The White Shadow. "I'll spare you your life if you promise to go back to Russia and never return," she compromised.

"It ain't over," The White Shadow said wincing in pain. The cold weather and rain were adding on to his injury. "We just getting started," he said in a pathetic attempt to sound tough. Angela may have defeated him physically, but he refused to be defeated mentally. "Come on bitch!" The White Shadow said moving in towards Angela.

"Quit while you're ahead," Angela warned. The White Shadow ignored Angela's warning and fired a weak hook that had no chance of landing or connecting with its intended target.

"Stop running from me, you scared ass bitch!" The White Shadow ran and attempted to kick Angela in the ribs. Angela easily caught The White Shadow's leg and swept his other foot from up under him sending him crashing down to the ground hard.

Angela watched sadly as The White Shadow slowly crawled back up to his feet and stumbled towards her. Once The White Shadow was in striking distance, Angela hit The White Shadow with a four-punch combination to the face, and then finished him off with a roundhouse kick to the head that put his lights out.

Angela slowly walked over to The White Shadow's unconscious body and used her foot to flip him over onto his stomach. She then kneeled down and grabbed The White Shadow's neck in a tight grip. She gave his neck a sickening twist to the right until a loud dramatic snapping sound could be heard.

Once it was all over, Angela collapsed down into the mud and stared up at the sky with her good eye. Her body felt like she had been involved in a bad car accident. Her body most definitely would need the proper amount of time to heal and recover after this episode.

Angela stared up at the sky and yelled, "He's gone! I took care of him for you like I promised... Do you forgive me now?" Angela continued looking up at the sky as if she was waiting for a reply to come back. After lying on the ground for a while, the rain suddenly stopped and out came the sun. Angela smiled. She took that as a sign from James up above responding to her question.

Angela slowly scrambled back up to her feet and made her way back inside the warehouse where she picked up her motorcycle, hopped on it, and burnt rubber peeling out of the warehouse like a bat out of hell. She didn't know where he was headed or what her next move would be. All she knew was that she was The Teflon Queen and now "The Number One Assassin in the World," a title she had definitely earned.

Epilogue

Six months later, Capo was finally released from the box and allowed back into regular population. After unpacking all of his belongings inside of his new cell, Capo's next stop was the yard. It had been a while since he was allowed to walk around freely so this was something he would have to get used to again. Capo coolly bopped through the yard with his head held high. He knew that the entire jail had been talking about the action packed movie he had made in the gym six months ago. Capo enjoyed putting in work, but what he didn't enjoy was the sad look on Kim's face when she had visited him in the box.

Kim was a good woman and the last thing Capo wanted was to disappoint or let her down. She had made him promise that once he was released from the box that he would stay out of trouble so that he wouldn't lose his good time and would still be able to make it home early on good behavior. Capo agreed to stay out of trouble, but what Kim didn't understand was that in jail, anything could happen and people fought and killed over the smallest things. He had made Kim a promise that he knew he couldn't keep. Kim would be mad, but hopefully she would forgive him.

Capo moved through the yard until he spotted Stacks and a few other Homies standing around talking shit to one another.

"What's good?" Capo asked giving everyone a pound.

"Looks like we got us a little problem on our hands," Stacks said and then nodded towards a bunch of mean looking men that stood in a group all wearing Kufic.

"Seems like ya man Cash done turned Muslim to keep us off his ass."

"Fuck him turning Muslim got to do with us?" Capo asked confused. He could care less what Cash had changed his religion to. When the two crossed each other's paths again it was on and popping on site.

"Nah... You don't understand. The Muslims are the biggest gang in the jail system. You fuck with one of them and a riot is sure to pop off," Stacks explained. He knew the aftermath of fucking with the Muslims and he didn't think it was worth taking it to a further extent with them, especially if it wasn't over money.

"Fuck that!" Capo spat. "And fuck them Muslim niggas... Shit done already went too far to stop now!" Capo could give two fucks about what organization Cash had joined. The fact still remained that lives had been lost and loved ones had been robbed and shot. It was already too turned up to turn down now. "What's up with that clown, Wayne?"

"He's paying the Muslims for protection," Stacks told him.

"You can't be serious," Capo said in disbelief. "Niggas is stone cold gangsta's on the streets and then come to jail and turn Muslim. Un-fucking believable!" He raved. As Capo sat talking, he noticed Cash and Wayne both enter the yard at the same time. Just the sight of Cash made Capo's blood boil. Yeah he had put hands and feet on him, but that wasn't enough. He wanted Cash to bleed. He wanted him to see what *real* pain felt like and he definitely wanted him to know this shit wasn't a game by no means what so ever.

Cash and Wayne were immediately flanked by Muslims when they entered the yard. They stood over in a huddle talking in hushed tones and every few seconds one of them would look back over his shoulder as if the organization was up to no good.

Capo didn't know what they were over there talking about, but if he had to guess more than likely, it was about him.

"Here we go," Stacks said out loud, as he noticed the gang of Muslims heading in their direction. Each man's face held a serious and dangerous no nonsense look on it. One of the Homies discreetly passed Capo a shank. When the two crews got within striking distance, the entire yard got quiet in anticipation of the violence that was sure to come next.

* * * *

Mr. Biggz sat in an expensive Italian restaurant with a beautiful black woman that wasn't his wife. He laughed, boasted, and bragged about how much money he had and how the world was all his.

The dark skin woman who sat across from Mr. Biggz laughing at every word that came out of his mouth. She was just happy to be in Mr. Biggz presence. She had been waiting for a while for Mr. Biggz to finally keep his word and take her out like the one he had promised so many times in the past. Now that she was actually spending time with him, she planned on enjoying herself.

"So tell me a little more about yourself," the dark skin woman that went by the name Shelly said as she sipped slowly from her glass of red wine.

"Well one word that can describe me is greatness," Mr. Biggz said arrogant and cockily. He had been on top for so long that he no longer knew how to be humble or how to appreciate things. In his world, it was either his way or the highway. His rules were simple. You could either love him or leave him alone.

"Greatness?" Shelly repeated just to make sure she had heard him correctly. "Define greatness."

"You're looking at it," Mr. Biggs replied shoveling a fork full of pasta in his mouth. "Let me explain something to you sweetheart." He took a sip of his drink and then continued. "You see in order to be great; you have to do great things."

"What have you done great lately?" Shelly challenged.

At first Mr. Biggz was about to answer Shelly's question and then he suddenly remembered that bosses didn't answer questions or explain themselves to no one, especially not a woman. "Listen bitch, I'm done answering these foolish questions. Sit down and shut up," he huffed. "Sit back and be thankful that I'm even allowing you to be around greatness."

"Nigga please!" Shelly shot back. "You must got me fucked up!" She stood up and tossed her drink in Mr. Biggz face and then stormed out of the restaurant leaving Mr. Biggz sitting there alone.

Mr. Biggz laughed an embarrassed laugh and then got up and headed towards the men's room.

He barged through the door with one thing on his mind. He couldn't wait to get home so he could make a phone call and get Shelly's head blown off for her disrespectful act.

As Mr. Biggz washed the red wine from his face, he heard a stall door behind him open and out stepped the one and only *"The Teflon Queen!"* Her face was covered in bruises. She wore all black, and in her hand rested a silenced 9mm.

"Angela," Mr. Biggz said as if he had seen a ghost.

"You don't look too happy to see me," Angela whispered. She knew her face was the last face he expected to see.

"Where's The White Shadow?" He asked.

"He's dead!"

"No way," Mr. Biggz said in disbelief. He just knew that The White Shadow would be able to easily defeat Angela any day of the week, even on his worst day.

"You've caused a lot of unnecessary bloodshed," Angela told him. "I lost a good man because of you."

"Fuck you!" Mr. Biggz growled. "That stupid ass man is who caused all of this!" He raved. "You met him and then you started changing... You are an assassin Angela! You can't be falling in love thinking you just gone ride off into the sunset. It don't work like that! You took a contract and didn't fulfill it. That's not my fault!"

"All the contracts I have done for you... You couldn't let one slide?" Angela fumed. "I've never asked you for nothing and then the first time I ask you for something, you put a contract out on me. That's how you do? I thought we was family?"

"Fuck family! This is business!" Mr. Biggz explained. He was a businessman and in his line of work, the word family was nonexistent. "You fucked up and went against the grain," he pointed out.

"I understand," Angela, said nodding her head. "I do, but what you're not understanding is that you took from me the only person that I've ever loved and the only person that ever loved me. Then I called you and asked you to dead this thing before it went too far."

"I'm sorry Angela. I'm not perfect, but I'll tell you what I'll do…"

Mr. Biggz brains exploded all over the mirror before he could finish his sentence. Angela stood over Mr. Biggz corpse and emptied the remainder of the clip in his body just for good measures.

Mr. Biggz was responsible for killing the one man who took Angela in when she was a kid and when no one else wanted or cared for her. He also responsible for killing the only man to ever love Angela for being herself and now she had finally got revenge. It was only right that she killed the man who had given her the name *"The Teflon Queen."* Mr. Biggz would always be a part of her because even if she didn't want to be, Angela would always be known as *"The Teflon Queen!"*

"The End… For Now"

Books by Good2Go Authors on Our Bookshelf

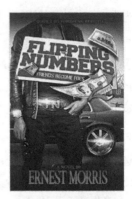

Teflon Queen 2

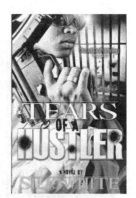

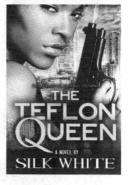

Silk White

Good2Go Films Presents

To order books, please fill out the order form below:

To order films please go to www.good2gofilms.com

Name: _____

Address: _____

City: _____ State: _____ Zip Code: _____

Phone: _____

Email: _____

Method of Payment: Check   VISA   MASTERCARD

Credit Card#: _____

Name as it appears on card: _____

Signature: _____

Item Name	Price	Qty	Amount
48 Hours to Die – Silk White	$14.99		
Flipping Numbers – Ernest Morris	$14.99		
He Loves Me, He Loves You Not - Mychea	$14.99		
He Loves Me, He Loves You Not 2 - Mychea	$14.99		
He Loves Me, He Loves You Not 3 - Mychea	$14.99		
Married To Da Streets – Silk White	$14.99		
My Boyfriend's Wife - Mychea	$14.99		
Never Be The Same – Silk White	$14.99		
Stranded – Silk White	$14.99		
Slumped – Jason Brent	$14.99		
Tears of a Hustler - Silk White	$14.99		
Tears of a Hustler 2 - Silk White	$14.99		
Tears of a Hustler 3 - Silk White	$14.99		
Tears of a Hustler 4- Silk White	$14.99		
Tears of a Hustler 5 – Silk White	$14.99		
Tears of a Hustler 6 – Silk White	$14.99		
The Panty Ripper - Reality Way	$14.99		
The Teflon Queen – Silk White	$14.99		
The Teflon Queen 2 – Silk White	$14.99		
The Teflon Queen – 3 – Silk White	$14.99		
The Teflon Queen 4 – Silk White	$14.99		
Time Is Money - Silk White	$14.99		
Young Goonz – Reality Way	$14.99		
Subtotal:			
Tax:			
Shipping (Free) U.S. Media Mail:			
Total:			

Make Checks Payable To: Good2Go Publishing - 7311 W Glass Lane, Laveen, AZ 85339

JUN 2020

CPSIA information can be obtained
at www.ICGtesting.com
Printed in the USA
LVHW021438160620
658247LV00021B/1578